Nick of Time

ROMENTICS

A Novel Approach To Gay Romance

***

Introducing a line of romance novels written just for gay men. It's all the steamy passion, crazy excitement and gay drama you'd expect when two men fall for each other—maybe even more. And they're all written with love by Scott&Scott.

***

Cover design by Jamie Allison
Authors' photo by Blakely Crawford

To order additional copies, please contact us.
BookSurge, LLC
www.booksurge.com
1-866-308-6235
orders@booksurge.com

SCOTT & SCOTT

NICK
OF TIME

A ROMENTICS NOVEL

www.Romentics.com
Log on and fall in love with Romentics.
2004

Nick of Time

CHAPTER 1

The last place Brent Sawyer expected to see beautiful shirtless boys was near his mother's house. Brent now lived down in New York—and you did not see the City's clubs, coffee houses, book stores, chic little storefronts crammed with modern design in rural Holmstead County where Brent had grown up. You did not see hot trashy Gucci boys and Banana Republicans. And you certainly did never saw a man like that.

The sudden glimpse of a mountain of rock-hard man-flesh by the side of the highway nearly caused Brent to drive his sporty blue Miata rental into an oak tree.

The guy was a massive stud. A walking pornographic fantasy—shirtless, lean, his chest carved from stone. He wore a pair of baggy carpenter jeans belted by a loose knot of rope slung low on his waist. He straddled one end of a stone wall at the edge of an open meadow, one boot on either side.

His shoulders bulged as he hefted a massive boulder, each muscle defined like an amateur anatomy lesson. The pants hung low enough so that Brett could see that even his butt muscles bulged with the effort.

His face was streaming sweat and deliciously filthy. He had full lips, a square-face and defined jaw and a butt-chin. His hair neatly cropped close to his head, but full and dark.

Brent could almost smell the musty crotch of the man, the fingernails crusted with grease. He was filthy. An animal. A gorgeous animal.

In the split second Brent zoomed by, the man looked up. Their eyes met. There was nothing in the world except that instant, powerful moment of mutual recognition and desire that gay men can share across a room, a street, a continent. It was magnetic. Electric. Hell, it was downright nuclear.

Only when Brent's tires left the pavement did Brent remember that he was speeding along at fifty miles an hour. The steering wheel jerked in his hands. The tires spun. The Miata shuddered. Its bumper passed within inches of a tree stump. Then his tires again found pavement. The back end fishtailed sickeningly and then fell into line.

When Brent checked the rearview, the man was gone. Lost around the bend in the road.

Brent slammed the brakes. His heart pounded. He was thinking that he should whip the car around. He should go back, engage this guy somehow. Chat him up. For the first time in his life, Brent could seriously imagine dragging this guy off the side of the highway and having sex in the open field, as if he were a stranger in a rest stop.

If only, he thought ruefully, *he had met more strangers like that when he was a horny kid in Holmstead County!*

A loud horn broke into the train of his fantasy. Brent had stopped in the middle of the road, and another car had come whipping around the corner. It swerved to avoid him.

Startled, Brent pulled to the side of the road.

Two near-death experiences in forty-five seconds, he thought. That was a world record. And all on account of a little bare flesh.

You're pathetic, Brent, he told his reflection in the rearview mirror. He had to get ahold of himself. This teenaged eagerness to find a man—any man—was exactly why he needed to go to his parents' place in the country and hang out for a week or two. He was just too hot and horny for his own good.

It was a good thing his sister Heidi had scheduled her wedding for the very same weekend Brent was fresh off breaking up with his boyfriend of six months. On the phone earlier that week, Brent had teased Heidi mercilessly about her timing. He had insisted that she ought to have foreseen his break-up and not hogged the whole weekend for herself. After all, she had been begging him to break up with Cory for months.

"Maybe you could re-book your wedding for a Wednesday, Heidi?" he had suggested.

"You'd better get your hot little buns up to Holmstead County as soon as you can, Brent," Heidi had responded, "or I'll chase you down in the city and drag you up by your boxer shorts."

Brent had surrendered to Heidi's vaunted skills of persuasion and headed home. Weddings, he thought irreverently, are hazardous to my health.

The calming influence of a few more miles of highway made Brent reflect that perhaps it was not such a bad idea for him to be away from all the available boys in New York City this weekend. Brent had been known in the past to bring the fine art of flirting to a nearly dangerous conclusion.

And this incident on the road, involving some random blue-collar dimwit who was probably not half so beautiful as the wishful glimpse had suggested and married and closeted with two kids besides—this incident only proved that it might not be such a bad decision to stay in the country a while until the flush of freedom wore off. Cold showers and long walks in the woods and boiled dinners and lots of straight people—this was a recipe for curing what ailed Brent. Which was good old-fashioned horniness.

But where had the stone man come from? Straight or gay, Holmstead County wasn't exactly a hotbed of Men's Fitness or Armani models. No one knows better than me, Brent thought, that fabulously hunky gay men were simply not bred here. With the exception—apparently—of this stone-tossing unicorn on the side of the road.

Brent passed the "Welcome to Sanbornton" sign that marked his hometown. The traffic was leisurely and Brent fell in behind a pickup towing a half-dozen all-terrain vehicles on a flatbed truck. The pickup could not seem to decide whether it would park or turn or drive on. It made infuriating brakes and stops and false turns. Brent was seething, jacked on city energy. It was all he could do to keep from leaning on the horn. When the pickup pulled over, Brent flashed the old man in the driver's seat a murderous glance. The old man gave him a friendly wave.

Brent took a pack of Camels from the glove compartment and shook one out. He indulged the smoking impulse only when driving long distance. Oh, well. Just one more bad habit that needed to change. He had already got rid of one bad habit—this last boyfriend Cory. Soon, he would work on the others. It was all part of a process.

Brent glanced at himself in the rear-view. His hair was brownish. The summer's bleach was fading away. It was cut short, but tousled and tufted by being in the open convertible. His face had a good bronze from the afternoon sun. It was thin, with a strong jaw and cheekbones, but the bones were light, graceful, almost delicate. He had been blessed with a bright, impish smile. Brent had never had trouble getting and holding the attention of men.

Still, Brent dismissed the stone man as a possible Mr. Right. He could admit to a thing for blue-collar boys, but he was sensitive to the economics of Mr. Right—and he was thinking that builders of stone walls in Holmstead County probably had not made the latest list of the Fortune 500. And, besides, even if the stone man had all the money in the world, the last thing he ever wanted to do was end up in his mother's hometown.

To go back permanently to Holmstead County—that would be the death of him. That would signify that Brent had surrendered all he had ever dreamed about since he was a little boy first beginning to suspect that he was different than all the rest. It would be as bad as the other dream he had squandered—the dream of a long career as a professional dancer. Which Brent had been forced to abandon after a promising start because of a freak injury to his knee that just would not heal right. Some things were just not meant to be.

Brent's mother's house was a lazy white Victorian set back on a little hill. A giant oak stood to one side and the lawn stretched back to rows of fruit trees. Brent's four sisters were playing badminton. His mother was leaning against the railing on the wrap-around porch. She began waving before he had even turned in the long driveway.

Brent's sisters clustered around the little sports car. The air filled with yelps and kisses. They extracted Brent from the interior and complained about cigarettes and told him how skinny and pretty he looked and tussled his already tussled hair.

There were four of them: Carrie, Hannah, Martha, and Heidi. All were older than Brent, with Heidi the closest to his age and his hands-down favorite. She understood him better than the rest.

Like him, Heidi had left Holmstead County for college. Brent had always dreamed that Heidi would come down to New York. That she and Brent would share an apartment together. That after Brent found his husband, he and she would be next-door neighbors. Conspirators. Companions. What better fag hag is there in the world, after all, than your own older sister?

But in the years after college had ended, Brent's father has passed away. Weeks later, their mother, too, had become ill. Heidi had returned to Holmstead County to care for her, and ended up staying on even after their mother's health had improved.

At the time, Brent had been bitterly disappointed. He was worried that Heidi was wasting her life. That she would end up alone back in Holmstead County, with no Brent, and no life, and no one but Carrie, Hannah, and Martha around for company.

Heidi, he had predicted, would never find somebody suitable here. She would end up settling for some man who was not worthy, and Brent would hate him.

But Heidi defied him as usual. She found an older man, Gar, who—as much as Brent had wanted to despise him—turned out to be kind and funny and handsome.

As Brent let himself be herded up the walk toward his mother, Heidi enveloped him in a big hug. She was whispering words of welcome he did not hear but somehow understood perfectly. There was a bond between them that was unlike any other, a language beyond words.

Brent's mother, Anita Sawyer, waited like a queen for him to come up the path to her. Brent's mother was every bit the matriarch, presiding over her flock and dominion.

Badminton game forgotten, the whole group flowed with Brent to the porch. They peppered him with questions, offers of iced tea, comments on his being too thin, and affectionate touches. They sat on the painted wicker on the front porch and gossiped about the wedding and the weather, and Mrs. Sawyer pointedly refused any questions about her health, which made all the kids tease her for being a martyr.

Then, out of the blue, Carrie looked at her watch and shrieked. The whole group of women, mother included, disappeared as if at four o'clock they were all going to turn into pumpkins.

Heidi was the last to go. She said, "So glad you're here, Brent." And then she, too, vanished.

Brent wandered inside and peeked into the dining room. He was flooded with warm memories of family dinners around the great oak table that had been passed through generations of Sawyers—and might someday be passed to him.

From the antique sideboard, Brent poured himself Bourbon over ice. The cubes rang hollowly in the bucket and the brown liquor made his eyes smart.

The screen door slammed and made him jump. It was his little brother, Adam, slouching in the doorway.

Adam drawled, "Whassup?" and then angled for the stairs.

"You too cool to stop to say hello, champ?"

"You want to pour me a drink, you could persuade me."

"Mom'd kill me."

Adam shrugged. "Then I got shit to do, dude."

"Not so fast, Sparky. I haven't seen you in six months. You're going to come down here and hang with your bro."

Brent added, "And don't even think about refusing. Remember-"

"Yeah, I remember—you changed my diapers. How could I forget? You remind me of that every time I see you."

Brent smiled. He corralled Adam's head in the crook of his

elbow and rubbed it. Adam howled and wrestled himself away and looked aggrieved on account of his hair.

The story was true. Brent *had* changed Adam's diapers. In fact, he had basically raised Adam from the time he was born until Brent left for school. Adam was seventeen, the child that had been a mistake, born fourteen years after Brent.

The boys lounged in the living room, side by side in chairs, legs sprawled. Brent asked him about girls, and school, and partying. Adam got animated and announced plans to be a millionaire by the time he was thirty—even if he did not yet have solid plans on how he would accomplish it.

"Invite me down to the city, dude," he said. "With a quickness."

"'With a quickness?' What's that? Dude-talk for 'quickly?'"

"Come on, dude. Soon as I turn eighteen, you gotta have me down, so me and my friends could meet some really hot girls."

"Your friends would be cool with…"

"It's cool, man. I told them you could party them under the table. They give you props for that."

As the sun fell, they laughed and shot the shit in the half-dark. Adam pestered Brent for a sip of Bourbon. Eventually, Brent supplied it. Adam choked it down, and announced that he would stick with beer in the future.

They were just getting comfortable when Mrs. Sawyer swept into the room, outfitted in a dress that looked like a ballroom gown.

"You boys aren't dressed?!" she scolded. She clucked and hustled them upstairs, making no distinction between the boy who was seventeen and the one who was thirty-one. "You two would be late for your own funeral!"

Adam and Brent looked at one another and shared a laugh and a sigh, and let themselves be reluctantly herded into suit and tie. That was the nice thing about home—you always got what you expected. It was familiar and comfortable—if not always the most exciting place in the world.

CHAPTER 2

Nick stood at the edge of the tarmac, where it crumbled into the road's shoulder. He yanked his shirt from his back pocket and used it to mop the sweat from his forehead. His muscles were sore. Pleasantly exhausted.

He stretched his arms above his head. Beads of sweat evaporated under the hot sun producing a sudden coolness like an unexpected caress. Nick extracted a water bottle from a hook on his belt and tipped up his head. The water spilled out into his mouth. It splashed over his face and down his neck in little rivulets that sped past his nipples, over his abdomen and found their way under his belt like frisky little fingers of teasing cold.

He gasped and shook his mane of thick, but close-cropped hair. Sweat and excess water spattered everywhere, as if he was a dog.

From the sun's angle, Nick gauged the hour and measured it against the progress he had made that day. He was satisfied with the day's work. He had moved, he estimated, upwards of two tons of stone.

Exactly on target. The project was moving according to schedule, on the plumb line he had laid out before beginning the work. Already he had built nearly a quarter-mile of wall along the edge of this meadow that a wealthy cardiologist from Boston planned to turn into his country estate.

The client was likely to be pleased. But more important, Nick was pleased. He had higher standards than most, and he was most happy when everything was going according to plan.

Call me old-fashioned, he thought. Plan ahead, and you don't have to keep stopping along the way to ask yourself if you're doing the right thing.

Nick had not always lived life according to plan. He had never cheated or lied to anybody in his life, but he had goofed around a bit in his early twenties. Because he had not been sure back then what he had wanted to do with his life, he hadn't done much. Certainly no heavy lifting. He had spent his days jetting around Boston on a bicycle with a pack of pierced and tattooed bicycle messengers. They had spent many of their nights partying in the clubs. Playing games. Killing time.

The only thing that had made him different from the rest of his companions was the vacations he had regularly taken from that life. He used to go up to the woods on his own, hitching rides up the thruway, until he reached some secluded spot where he read and drank water and swam naked in mountain lakes for three days at a time.

Nick was not the kind of man who had many regrets, and he did not regret this vagabond interlude. He figured he had drawn lessons from it and these lessons had made him a better man.

He had learned, among other things, that most people—like the bike messengers—were not up to his standards or expectations. Most did not have half his energy. Or curiosity. Or his ability to follow a project through to its end.

Nick figured that if he ever found a person who could match him in these ways, he would hang on to that person tight. That person should be treasured like a precious stone. At one time, the search for this mythical person had been all that had animated him. Hard experience changed that. He had mistaken too much costume jewelry for diamonds. For the real thing. He had been burned. Badly. Falling in love with Alex.

Alex had been a talker like Nick's father, a nonstop stream of quip and tease and ferment. He had been feminine and lithe, angelic and beautiful. In his cheek had been the blush of youth that made him seem fired up.

Nick had mistaken this transient beauty for character, fervor for genuine ambition, flattery for shared goals. Alex had enjoyed Nick's attentions, ridiculed his past times, and professed to be in love, to share a dream. He told Nick that they would always walk arm-in-arm, when they were old and frail. Nick had begun by seducing, and ended up seduced.

Nick took him in, rented an apartment with him, and began a life. After two years of growing increasingly bored of playing house, Alex began telling increasingly obvious lies. Nick had given him second chances. Offered him a way out. Excused indiscretions.

Alex used this permissiveness to his advantage. He was still cheating, and still charming, and finally he had left.

His departure marked a turning point. It seemed inexplicable afterward to Nick how he could have been drawn to Alex in the first place. The self-deception to which Nick had succumbed was an undeniable weakness. Something to guard against.

Nick buried his dream of finding an equal. A partner. He became disciplined. Trained his body. Trained his mind. He declared that he would never fall in love, a claim he made only to himself. So that, if by some miracle it should occur again, he would not be found to be a liar. Nick was scrupulously honest with others, but not always, he recognized, with himself.

The experience with flighty Alex taught him a lesson. He had learned that he didn't want things that would not fly away from you at the very first gust of wind. He liked creating things with his hands, weighty things, that had permanence and beauty.

Nick surveyed the half-built wall. This will be here forever, he thought. I can come back to it at any time. It will be here long after I am gone, long after anybody remembers my name.

He smiled grimly, and emptied the remainder of the bottle over his head. He gathered his few things from the work site.

His trade required few tools, other than his own bare hands. He did not have to rely on anything but himself. Or bad employees. If he succeeded, the success was his alone; if he failed, he had no one else to blame. That was how it should be.

Nick hopped into the cab of his oversized black pickup, with its long bed in back. He could probably even have dispensed with the pickup truck, too, truth be told. Cut back to the absolute minimum of tools. The bare bones.

But the clients expected such a manly truck from someone in his trade. They expected such a truck from a man of his size. Because he met their expectations, they were more likely to hire and trust him. The pickup truck was simply one more part of the costume. It was not really false advertising, or misleading. He was every bit as good at his trade as the part he played.

It was the peaceful part of the New England afternoon. The sun turned gold, and stillness set in over the meadows. The only sound was the grasshoppers and other busy insects, who, Nick liked to think, never took a moment off from building their own walls. This, he thought, was all the camaraderie and fellowship he needed in the world. Solitude and stones and the companionship of worker bees were so much better than the cheap relationships that others counted as friendships and civilization and life.

Several times that day, the tinny thumping of cars from the city had disturbed Nick. They drove too fast with the stereo turned too high. They were outsiders. Unimportant. Transient. Gone in no time.

They were probably passing through to other places, or up to visit. Perhaps, he thought, they were even there to attend the wedding of Heidi Sawyer.

He hoped not. Nick liked and admired Heidi. And he had always thought there was something plastic, something synthetic about these people from away. They had too much of everything, got bored of it too quickly, and turned to something new without really having understood or appreciated the old. They did not learn to want what they had, but only wanted what they had not. They were not of Heidi's caliber and he hoped she would not lower herself by entertaining their friendship.

Despite all Nick's justified contempt, he could admit that one of them had caught his eye at an unthinking moment—a hottie zipping by in his tiny Miata, sunglasses on his head, hair tousled, chest bared to the summer sun. He had been youthful-looking, with a blush of rose in his cheek and a small frame, but his fine bare shoulders had been broad enough to suggest that he was man enough for Nick.

Nick felt sure, too, that the boy had looked back at him. No surprise in that. People looked at him all the time. He stood a head taller than most men and had a solid frame. He was proud of his body, but not vain. He did not work out for the looks and praise that his appearance won from strangers, neighbors, and even the lonely wives of his customers, who many times he had to gently dissuade from coming on to him.

Not that there was anything wrong with a pretty face. The boy in the Mazda had been pretty. Very pretty. Like a bauble. A trinket. Something that in his past life—before Alex—he might have been quick to want to play with.

Now, Nick had other, greater concerns than foolish boys. He had had his fill of pretty baubles. He would have a family soon. Two girls and a boy. A wife. He had it all planned out, and nothing would get in the way.

Nick thought back again over the day's work, and thought proudly that he had made much progress, and yet had much further to go. But he had no doubt, no doubt at all, that he would finish what he had started. Period. Once and for all.

CHAPTER 3

The rehearsal dinner got off to a rocky start. Brent and Adam managed to defy their mother's scolding. They appeared ten minutes late delaying dinner. Their tardiness won them dark looks from Gar's side of the family, whose eyes were like embers in the stone fireplace.

"Are they hungry, or something?" Brent whispered to Heidi. It was a wonder to Brent that these stiff people could possibly be related to Heidi's fiancé, who was sweet and patient and an all around good guy.

Heidi tersely directed Brent to his chair, positioned he noticed at a fair distance from any of Gar's relatives.

"She's trying," he explained to Adam, who was similarly banished, "to break them in slow."

The tense stand-off lasted all dinner long, and Adam and Brent shared dour looks with each other, imitating the other side of the table, until they both had to excuse themselves, they were cracking up so much.

Fortunately, things improved after dinner. They cleared out the tables and chairs and the starched linen and uniformed servers from the grand dining room of the inn, replacing them with a DJ, an amplifier, and some strobe lights. The flashing lights made the pastoral hunting scenes on the wallpaper dance and the chandeliers jiggle and sway. The DJ, who had been brought up from the city, cranked up the music until the old inn was shaking on its foundations.

Guests started arriving, in clumps and gobs, further adding to the mood and diluting the tension between the families. Heidi had planned a huge party so that she could keep the wedding and reception down to just close friends and family.

Brent abandoned himself to a frenzy of dancing. First he began with his sisters. Their reluctant husbands were only too happy to be rid of the chore. One after another, and sometimes two at once, Brent whirled his sisters around the floor.

Eventually, he got enough courage to ask members of Gar's family. They surrendered themselves with looks of fear, but eventually gave in to the good time he showed them. He lost himself in the lights and the pulse of the music. At one point he pulled Adam out on the floor. A few stolen beers had made Adam shed the bulk of his self-consciousness, and he proved to have—to his surprise and Brent's—Brent's gifts for athleticism and movement.

"Watch that knee!" Heidi warned.

"Yes, Mom," Brent shot back and promptly did a full split on the floor at Adam's feet.

As they grew more frenzied, a little circle of people crowded around him. He seized Heidi from the margin. Heidi was the tall one in the family, lithe and willowy. She made her hips shake and tremble, yanked her formal dress up around her knees and began a bump and grind that brought them both to the floor and back. The crowd clapped and cheered.

Then Heidi took up a position in the middle, austere but with gently rolling hips, hardly moving. Brent danced up a storm around her, between and under legs, shimmying around her waste like a man electrified. Heidi was still and demure, one end of her formal dress bunched in her hand, as if she was the center of the solar system and Brent was all the planets.

Brent was so intent on their dancing and this little circle of fame and adulation that had gathered around them, and so shining with love for his sister, that he did not at first see the broad, dour figure looming in the entrance to the grand dining room next to the French doors.

The figure did not enter the room. He was scowling as if all this light and smoke and commotion were enough to drive him away. His eyes had fixed on the dancers in the center of the room; he was tall enough to see over the crowd around them.

It was the stone man!

There was no mistaking the charged energy between them as his eyes locked with Brent's. It was as if the crowd had cleared away and opened a vast corridor with them at either end.

"It's the stone man!" Brent blurted. Brent was so firmly frozen in place, that he did not notice that his sister had laid herself out for a luxurious deep dip, and he almost dropped her.

"Brent!" she scolded, having managed to catch herself before hitting the hardwood.

"Sorry, Heids, I got distracted."

Heidi threw a furious glance at him. "Just what I need on the eve of my wedding," she scolded. "A broken back!"

She glanced over her shoulder toward the entryway to see what had won Brent's attention. A light dawned over her face. She shook her head and pursed her lips.

"I should have known," she shouted over the blare of the music. "I know that kind of distraction."

Brent had the grace to blush. It was true that he had been bad when he was younger. His eyes had been out of control, lighting on anything with a swinging dick. He had been known to lose track of conversations, of any sense of dignity or proportion, to drop his jaw and bug his eyes. Nothing had existed but the men in the room.

Brent hoped he was over the flood of hormones that had ruled his youth. It was not like he slept with just anybody. He just liked a good flirt as much as the next guy, that was all.

And besides, he thought, this was different. This magnetism between him and the stone man was more powerful than any hormonal surge. It came from the gut, a powerful, almost tidal draw.

"Don't get your hopes up," Heidi warned.

"What?"

"Don't get your hopes up. He's next in line for getting hitched. He and his fiancée have this place booked for next month."

"Him?!! Married?! He's queer as a three-dollar bill."

Heidi's face hardened. She shrugged. She had many times lectured Brent about pigeonholing people into gay and straight "straitjackets," as she put it. Which, Brent thought, was about what you would expect from a woman who had munched her fair share of rug in college and still felt just the slightest bit guilty on behalf of her sex for the rank betrayal of having decided that she preferred men.

Heidi drew him off the dance floor to the corner bar.

"Look," she lectured sternly, "I'm only telling you what the facts are. And the fact is, you won't get far with him. He's marring a, well, a *wonderful* girl, and that's that. Case closed."

Brent looked at her fondly. In thirty years of fighting with her, he had never won an argument cleanly yet.

"I mean it," she said.

He glanced back at the door. Nick had not moved. He was beautiful. A powerful, undeniable presence in the room. He stood six-foot-four inches at least, broad in the chest, a stone warrior, a marble colossus, guarding the door. It was almost as if Nick himself were made out of the building blocks of his occupation—a hard, sculpted presence.

The play of dance lights over his face brought out the angles and shadow. He looked ruddy, fit, and leonine.

"Dance with me!" Brent again snatched at Heidi.

She refused. "You're dangerous, right now. I'd like to be sure that there's someone there to catch me when I dip, thank you very much."

"I'll dance!" one of Brent's cousins interjected. She shoved Heidi aside and threw herself into Brent's arms. They immediately began a series of close, hip-grinding moves that raised the temperature in the room.

Nick had moved from the door toward the bar. But he was still looking at Brent with lightning flashes of disapproval.

And I haven't even taken my shirt off yet, Brent thought with a smile.

Other people's disapproval only made him want to get more naughty.

His cousin, who had noticed the electricity between Brent and Nick, begged to be let in on the secret. Brent told her that Nick seemed to disapprove of their dancing, so she immediately adjusted her dress so more cleavage could show.

When the song ended, Brent broke for the bar. Nick watched him approach with a look of candid interest. His eyes moved from Brent's head down to his crotch and back up again. It was a blistering look, all heat and ferocity, rudeness and muscle.

Brent added a little extra strut to his walk. He knew he looked good. Dancing had made him hard and lean.

"Hello, there," he said, making it clear he had not come to the bar for a drink.

"Hello," Nick answered shortly.

It was all Brent could do to breathe. Nick's face was chiseled. His pecs bloomed beneath his open-necked shirt. The hand on his glass was like a shovel, the fingers long and thick. His eyes were clear and full of intelligence, and yet there was something dirty about him, something hidden and sexual, coiled in him like a spring.

"Friend of the bride? Or the groom?"

"Heidi's. You must be her gay brother." He said it dismissively, mouthing the word "gay" the way he might have referred to Adam as Heidi's "little" brother.

"Well, usually I just use the term brother, since she has no straight brothers."

"What about Adam?"

"Oh, details, details. He doesn't count. He's like seventeen years old. I meant adult gay brothers. Men. Like you and me."

Nick nodded.

"I've heard about you," Nick finally said, very quietly.

"What have you heard?" Brent asked, playfully.

Nick's sharp blue eyes flickered up at him like a tongue of flame.

"Everything."

"I doubt you've heard everything. A girl's got to keep some secrets to herself."

Nick's mouth twisted in disgust, as if the use of the term 'girl' had mortified some deeply held almost religious principle. This one, Brent thought, was about as buttoned up as they come.

"You want a drink?"

Nick pointedly raised his glass.

"I meant another drink."

"Thank you, no, I prefer not to overindulge."

"You want to dance?"

"I don't dance."

Brent reached for the hand closest to him. "Of course you do. Everybody dances!"

Nick snatched his hand away.

"I don't dance," he repeated. "And I never say something I don't mean." He turned back to his drink as if Brent was not there.

Brent studied him, a little flush in his face. Normally he would not be so bold, but the man's obvious interest in Brent's body and his behaving like an utter dickhead made Brent want to tweak him. Punish him. Take him for a ride.

"Would you like to have sex, then?" he proposed. "Do you indulge in sex?"

The disapproval that had been lurking in the background crept into Nick's eyes. He turned his head with reptilian slowness, opened his mouth as if to answer, and then thought better of it.

"Come on," Brent demanded impatiently, "don't you act so prissy with me, Mr. Stone Man. We both know why I'm asking."

"Actually," Nick said, "I'm waiting for my fiancée."

Brent laughed. "Come on, my friend. You might fool the rest of them. *I* know better."

Nick shifted his weight from one foot to the other. Brent felt as if some massive powerful perhaps dangerous animal had shifted in its sleep. He felt the thrill of a delicious fear at this whiff of danger. His whole body felt electric and alive.

"Are you some kind of closet case?" he persisted, knowing that he was probably going too far.

Nick signaled the bartender for another drink.

"Are you?" Brent persisted, pressing closer, close enough that they could have fit in a phone booth together.

"Do you always pry into people's personal lives within thirty seconds of making their acquaintance?"

"Only when they want me so bad that they can't hide it."

"Physical attraction is meaningless," Nick lectured. "I'm looking for something more." His weird, philosophical tone had more place in a convent than at a bar.

"I'll give you something, more, trust me. I've never had any complaints in that department," Brent boasted.

Nick sniffed and turned his body away from Brent.

A sign of denial? Of rejection? Or did he want Brent to get a better view of his fine, muscled ass?

Brent could not decide.

But what he *did* know was that all the electricity that had passed between them was now charging up his relentless inner bitch. It was not simply the pique of rejection. There was some other pompous, stubborn quality that made Brent want to plague him relentlessly. Get his goat. Raise his ire.

He was beginning to hate this guy.

"Get over yourself, cowboy," Brent snorted. "You aren't as special as you think you are. That's the problem with these rural places. You get an exaggerated idea of your own prettiness. In the city, you realize, pretty is a dime a dozen."

Anger burned in Nick's eyes. Nick clenched a fist. It looked like he wanted to put his hand around Brent's neck.

For a moment, a delicious spark of fear passed through Brent, down his spine, made his toes tingle as if they itched to race away some place safe. But it was exactly the reaction Brent had been searching for.

"Hey, forgive me for knowing what I want, guy," he said. "I guess I made a mistake. I mistook you for human."

And then, with only a sharp, sardonic glance in Brent's direction, Nick was gone. At first Brent thought he had driven Nick out, but his triumph was premature. At the door to the grand dining room, Nick took the hands of a lost-looking woman who was standing there. She had ivory-white skin and jet-black hair that she tucked behind one ear. She was pretty in a reserved, scholarly way, like a librarian who had taken off her severe cat-glasses and was now ready to party.

Nick whispered something in the woman's ear. Her eyes swept the bar and focused on Brent.

Brent felt stupid. Awkward. Exposed. He blew out a long, empty sigh. It was not how he had expected the encounter to go. What had started out as fun had ended with him getting dissed.

Brent watched them cross the room to his sister, who was sitting in a window seat like a queen on a throne, receiving well-wishers and guests.

Heidi embraced the couple wholeheartedly, first the woman, and then Nick, in whose arms Heidi seemed as small as a little girl. Brent found himself jealous of his sister. Those arms, he thought, belong to me!

The women chattered excitedly, but Nick did not speak. His eyes were restless. He looked as if he would have liked to begin hoisting stones right then and there and built a wall around himself.

Nick stole a glance back at him. The heat was unmistakable. But having been caught, Nick looked away immediately, and did not again succumb to the temptation.

Yet Brent sensed that he knew exactly where Brent was in the room. It was like hackles raised on the back of his neck.

As soon as Heidi had finished greeting another pair of well-wishers, Brent bee-lined across the room to his sister.

"Are you having fun?" she asked.

"You're friends with them? I mean, Nick and his beard."

"Yes." Her tone was guarded.

"But don't you see that marriage is the biggest joke in the history of the world?!"

Heidi took a moment to gather her thoughts. When she spoke, she spoke with careful deliberation, as if this was a matter on which she had already reflected, and long since made her peace.

"You know, Brent, this may be a novel idea, but why don't you get some facts before you start making judgments of a situation, ok?"

"Facts?! What facts do I need?! The guy's a big fucking queen and he's pretending that he's in love with that iceberg of a woman! Those are the facts."

"That iceberg is a friend of mine."

"No problem. I'm sure she's great. But she's marrying a queer!"

"Keep your voice down!"

Gar sashayed up to them in a giddy mood.

He said, "Hmmm…. flared nostrils, bright red faces…let me guess that you two Sawyers have already found something to disagree about." He looked at his watch. "Right on time. I knew you two couldn't go six hours without getting cranky."

"I didn't start it," Heidi said. "It's his fault."

"Heidi," Brent explained to Gar, "has trouble confronting the truth. I don't know if you noticed that."

Heidi flounced off. "I'll leave him to you, Gar. He's absolutely impossible!"

They both watched her go.

"What's the sore spot this time? Or should I ask?"

"Nothing. It's just…. What's up with this guy, Nick? What's his story?"

He nodded over at Nick. He was unmistakable in the flashes of disco light, his hands in his pockets, grim as a gargoyle.

"Nick's a friend of your sister's. I don't know him very well. Nice enough guy, doesn't talk too much. They say he's brilliant. We're going to their wedding next month," he added brightly.

"He's gay."

"No, they're getting married. They've been engaged almost a year."

"Don't play naive with me."

Gar looked wounded. "No, really. They're getting married. I'm sure of it. He's not gay."

Gar seemed so genuinely convinced of this that Brent fell silent, amazed that people could not see what he was seeing. Or chose not to see it. Conveniently. With, he thought, that kind of total obtuseness breeders adopt when it comes to kids and marriage.

"It's really a romantic story," Gar continued energetically. "She's Irish, you know. The woman. She came to this country seven years ago with her husband. He was killed, and his green card and work visa wasn't transferable. But Nick was one of her good friends—he took her in and helped her out. And they fell in love. And now, because she's getting married, she'll be able to stay over here, too! Become a citizen!"

Gar's eyes shone as he spoke. Brent wondered how many drinks he had had.

"That's quite a story," Brent agreed bitterly. "A real *fairy* tale."

Gar did not get the joke.

"I really admire him," Gar said solemnly, "for being willing to take on the kids."

"Kids?!!"

"Yes, she's got three. And Nick, I mean, he could have the pick of any girl he wanted in the Valley."

"Or any guy."

"Nick had the strength of character not to be blinded by the added burden."

"Blind's a good word."

Gar finally recognized the sarcasm in Brent's voice. He looked at Brent with a sad, pious and understanding expression. Laying a hand on his shoulder, he said, "I'm sorry it didn't work out with that boy you were dating. Heidi told me."

"Ah, good riddance!" Brent said automatically, until he realized that Gar thought he was just conjuring up gay men where they did not exist on account of Brent's broken heart. Brent nearly gacked. Flabbergasted that he should be the object of Gar's pity. That anyone could think he was in need of reassurance.

"You'll find the right man," Gar said.

"Of course I'll find the right man. I'm hot, remember?!"

Gar went off after to Heidi. Dejected and restless, Brent fetched a drink and returned to his dancing. Suddenly, he was ready for both this night and the whole weekend to be over, so that he could safely go home. Where at least people dressed more tastefully.

Mrs. Sawyer caught him in a corner dancing by himself.

"Brent!" she scolded, "If you keep that hangdog look on your face someday it's going to stay there!"

"I certainly hope so. Then, maybe, no one will talk to me, and I won't get annoyed with people."

"BRENT!"

"Not you, Mama." He laughed and kissed her on the cheek, making an effort to break out of his gloom for her sake. "You can always talk to me."

"Well, I should think so! I'm your mother."

"And a fine mother you be!" He threw his arm around her and smoothed her ruffled dignity.

"Are you enjoying your sister's party?" Her voice contained a warning, indicating that the right answer was yes.

"Of course I am, mother. Of course, of course, of course. I'm just having that acute stranded feeling we gay men feel from time to time when we get into a situation crammed with breeders and there's not a nancy queen in sight with whom to dish. Even the bartenders are straight for God's sake!"

His mother smiled bravely. "We 'breeders' are hard to abide, aren't we?"

"Amen!"

"Oh, dear, I didn't know you had taken up religion again! I'm so pleased!"

Brent gave his mother a cross-eyed look. He had not won

his bitchery out of thin air. It was in his genes, straight from her womb.

Brent hugged her affectionately.

"I can't win with you, Ma. And you know what?"

She eyed him warily.

"I don't think of you as a breeder anyway. With that kind of attitude, you can be an honorary gay man."

She laughed, shook her head, and they fell into a mutually appreciative silence, arms linked. Together, they were like a fortress wall.

"So..." Brent said finally. "Give me the dish on this Irish girl and the stone guy." Brent knew he could count on his mother to be privy to all the county gossip.

She led Brent out into the hall where she would not have to shout over the music. "I think it's all very romantic," his mother said carefully.

Brent gave her a hard look right back. He knew his mother. She was very practical. Being 'romantic' usually meant that she disapproved of it.

He leaned over and kissed her on the cheek.

"I'm glad you're on my side, Ma."

"I'm not on anyone's side, dear. I wasn't aware there were sides."

"Oh, there are always sides, Mama."

"Have another biscuit," she urged, reaching for the tray of sugar cookies someone had left out on the side table.

CHAPTER 4

Nick was furious with himself. He knew he would not sleep. That little tart had been talking about him! He just knew it! He had been talking about Nick with everyone at the party, and it drove Nick crazy not to know what had been said.

He knew that he should have had more control. He never should have gotten drawn into that conversation in the first place. That tart had no idea of the consequences of his own actions or speeches, or gossip. Or, more likely, he was so self-centered he just did not give a damn. Like every guy Nick had ever known, he was only concerned about how he looked and his own momentary appetites. He did not have any concept of the things that mattered in life. The foundations.

And now, to top it off, Una was angry. She would not admit to it. Anger would have been unreasonable, and Una was always reasonable. Always. No matter what. He had never seen her lose her temper or complain more than a problem deserved.

She had seen far worse than this in her day. The death of Fergus, the father of her children. Her disastrous love affair with Peter, a man Nick—to his undying regret and embarrassment—had introduced her to. A visit from an immigration agent, harassing her for papers. It looked like her life was over, and she and her children would be deported to Ireland, where they had nothing—no house, no family, no love.

Throughout all these calamities, she had kept her wits about her. Nerve once showed anger. Only reasoned through the situation and picked the course most likely to keep her safe.

Una had done the same now. She had developed a convenient case of cramps and had demanded that Nick take her home early.

Now, she was either asleep in the passenger seat, or pretending. Nick was driving the great white pickup home under a moonless night sky. A deer was feeding by the roadside and it bounded into the woods as they approached.

He glanced at Una, the fondness rising up in his chest. He admired her as a partner and friend and mother. Her main, overriding concern was always her children, first and foremost, and Nick had always admired this dedication. If she had a fault, it was being overzealous in looking out for the ones she loved.

Nick had not minded leaving Heidi's party early, of course. The room had reeked of sloppy habits. It had been too loud to permit a decent conversation. Loud, drunken, promiscuous parties were not really his thing. Heidi would hardly have expected them to stay long. Especially, he consoled himself, with the kids at home. And Nick having to work tomorrow.

The thought of work and children reassured Nick. The churning in his stomach subsided and his racing thoughts slowed. Work and children meant responsibility. Stability. The things he had always wanted out of life. That anybody with any wisdom wanted out of life.

Kids, marriage, love. They fit together like a row of stones. Solid. Righteous. He thanked God for having brought Una into his life. She gave him exactly what he needed. And he owed it to her, after introducing her to Peter.

From the day they met, Una and Nick had immediately realized that they shared an intense curiosity and were interested equally in every topic under the sun. Una seemed to understand the satisfaction Nick got from stone. They had discovered they shared the same values, the same desire for family, the same fierce loyalty to friends.

The relationship made Nick's father proud. Una was one of his students, and he once said to Nick, "I knew you two would get along." Another time, he said, "I know you better than you think."

At the time, Nick had finished his apprenticeship and started in business. He had hired a promising young man to help him.

A guy named Peter. In an effort to do something good for Una, Nick introduced her to his worker, a promising young man on whom Nick himself had a bit of a crush. The coworker had got her pregnant, promised to marry her, and then run off.

It was Una who pointed out after Peter that she did not need another man like him. Another romantic involvement. She needed a life partner.

Nick had never before considered what she was suggesting. But the logic was undeniable. Each of them could provide the other what they were looking for: security. Stability. Balance. Within a week, Nick had proposed. There may not have been sparks and lightning strikes, but they were made for one another. Affectionate and respectful.

Yet, for all that, Nick could not keep his thoughts from returning to that boy on the dance floor—that lean body under the teasing light, the graceful movements interspersed with the vain deliberate provocations, the flashes of skin. The *thrust* of him, the rounded ass that boy used like a flag in front of a bull.

It was intolerable. Watching this boy throw his lean, hard body around, putting himself on display—It was profligate. Promiscuous. Reckless. Wasteful.

These words shot into his head like bullets, and they were all curse words to Nick. The things he most detested in the world. What rewards could they possibly hold when held up against kids, marriage, and love?

He was undoubtedly sexy, Nick would allow him that. Young, too—a few years younger than Nick himself. He still had that feverish blush in his cheeks, like a teenage boy. Nick's throat went dry just thinking of it. His crotch tightened with the most obvious and degrading sense of want and desire he had felt in years.

But then, just when Nick might conclude Brent was not so bad, there would be a bump and a grind, a leer and a wink, all of it—Nick felt certain—somehow meant to torment Nick.

He was surprised at the strength of his disapproval. What some stranger did with his life ought to have been a matter of no concern to him. The boy was a lightning flash in the County. He would be gone in no time, and then things would be the same again.

Una stirred in the seat beside him. "What are you thinking about?" she asked.

The question caught Nick off guard. Neither he nor she was particularly talkative, and they often went long comfortable stretches with one another without a word.

It took him a moment to form the words.

"I was just thinking how annoyed I was with that gay man that was there at the party." It did not occur to him to say different. Lying was not a habit that Nick had an instinct for. He always said what he thought, without thinking, and he hoped he always would, no matter what consequences followed. He detested liars.

"You didn't look much annoyed," Una observed. She shook a smoke from her pack, lit it, and cracked the window.

Nick winced. It was her only habit that he did not approve of. That they did not see eye to eye on.

"No?"

"No. More...star-struck." Her lips massaged the word into a warm, round coo. Even after so many years in the United States, she hadn't lost a trace of her Irish accent. It was as thick as if she had just come from the fields of Limerick, and he thought it was the most beautiful sound in the world.

"I guess I'm not used to seeing city people. He reminded me of Al-...."

"I know," she said. "I know he did." Her hand reached out and fell on his thigh, and he enjoyed the pleasant warmness of it.

Una had always been good that way. The smallest gesture from her was a balm. It was no surprise that she should see in Brent what he had—that striking shadow impression of his old lover, Alex. Who had also been a flirt. Like Brent, Alex had been an electric wire. People were drawn to him like moths to a flame.

Nick now knew he was just one more drawn by the flame and ultimately burned.

The experience had, Nick acknowledged, made him a little

bitter. But a little wiser, too. And this, he thought, probably explained why he had such a negative reaction to Brent.

I've got a serious weakness. I'm like a crow, he thought. *I see something shiny and I want to pick it up. But the better character inside of me knows better. Sees more clearly.*

Discipline, he told himself. That was what it took to overcome this. He had to keep his eyes on the prize.

Nick looked over at Una and smiled warmly in the dark. If nothing else, Una knew what commitment was. What discipline was. She understood what he was talking about.

Una caught his smile and slid over on the seat next to him, beneath his arm. Again, he thought that they were safe. It was all going according to plan.

CHAPTER 5

Brent was trying to remain friends with the bride on her wedding day. He was in her bedroom, hanging out with bridesmaids, and drinking Mimosas. They were gossiping about who had kissed whom at the party the night before. Who had been caught doing the walk of shame back to the hotel at dawn.

Heidi was in front of the mirror, trying on her dress.

Still talking and gossiping, Brent slipped up behind her, worrying her dress, making subtle adjustments to the fall of the cloth and the positioning of the flowers.

She slapped away his hands. "Enough already!"

"What? I'm just trying to make you beautiful."

"Stop trying so hard. It's not flattering."

Brent smiled. His sister was nervous. It had been a long time since he had seen her like that.

She looked at him and took a deep breath. Her eyes were as large as he had ever seen, but he also saw that she knew he understood her.

"Another Mimosa!" he declared, and the bridesmaids fell into a flurry of mixing, spilling champagne and making everybody laugh.

Brent took Heidi's hand, which was cold.

"Gar's a damn lucky guy," he murmured.

Heidi smiled. A tear dropped down her face. "You bastard," she said. "Some day you're going to be doing this, too, and I'm going to make you cry."

Brent grinned. They hugged—gently, so as not to disturb the dress.

Then came the knock at the door—it was Adam announcing

the car was ready. Brent seized Adam by the lapels and dragged him into the room.

"Let them wait!" he shouted.

And he and Heidi and the bridesmaids fussed with Adam's tuxedo, until he turned bright red. The bridesmaids all pretended to swoon and remarked on how handsome he was, and plied him with champagne, until Adam was beet-red and giggling.

"Men are so easy," Brent sighed. "The way they give into feminine wiles."

"Not all men!" piped up Adam, attempting to reassert some of his dignity.

"Most."

"Most," he acknowledged. And then added slyly, "Like that guy Nick last night."

Everybody in the room froze. Heidi shot Adam a look as dark as a storm cloud.

"What about him?" Brent asked warily.

"His wife played him like a sucka. 'I've got a headache....' Boohoo. She's cramping his style."

Heidi looked relieved, but she shot Brent an accusing glance.

"He said it, not me," Brent said. Then he leaned over and whispered dramatically in Adam's ear, "I'll give you that check later on."

"Nick's style isn't partying," Heidi said primly, ignoring the taunt. "So it's not like she just dragged..."

"He's BORING," Adam declared, interrupting her.

"He's dreamy," gushed one of the bridesmaids. Her face was flushed with alcohol.

"He's very dedicated to his work," Heidi said primly.

"Bor-ring," Adam repeated in a singsong. His eyes were on the bridesmaid, whom he was trying to impress.

"What work?" Brent asked.

"He's a stone mason. He lays stone walls. The old-fashioned way, without mortar or anything. Just balancing the stones one on the other, hundreds of them. He's really quite good."

"Oh," Brent said. He had been expecting some secret Picasso or something. "Just walls?"

"Or whatever. Bridges. Tunnels. Don't look so superior," she said. "It's quite a lucrative business from what I hear. People come to him from all over New England. He used to go off on jobs for weeks at a time. That is, before he and Una settled down. Now people from away are buying vacation homes in the county—they've got gobs of money and all want to pretend they have estates that have been in the family for generations. So he builds stone walls for them, and he can charge whatever he wants. He hardly ever has to leave the county any more." She leveled her gaze at Brent. "Lucky for his wife."

Brent did not take the bait. "Your lucky it's your wedding day, smart ass."

The wedding was a powerful, intimate affair. They exchanged vows that they had written and Brent had stood proudly in front of the church as one of Gar's ushers. At the reception, Brent had delivered a long humorous toast in the form of a rhyming poem that had brought the house down.

At the end of the reception, when Heidi and Gar left, Brent had to escort his sobbing mother back to her home. Long after she went to bed, he sat up alone on the porch of the house he had grown up in, beneath a giant rural night sky that was impossibly filled with stars.

Brent let his thoughts roam without hurry. He thought about the future he now faced. His sister's choices. The choices others made.

From the distant highway came the low howl of an eighteen-wheeler driving off into the night. Leaves rustled in the trees, and somewhere a car door slammed. A dog barked.

Brent had forgotten the long slowness of a rural summer night. He had gotten used to heat of the club, the noisy bustle of rooftop dinner parties fueled with bitchy repartee and alcohol. The bruising caffeinated brunches the morning after.

But at that moment, on the porch of his old family home, with just a vague lingering high from the reception, none of that city life seemed so full as a summer night in Holmstead County.

He sighed contentedly and put his feet up on a wicker ottoman. The only other thing he could wish for was a bare-chested man with a ten-inch cock to share the moment with.

He was joking with himself of course. (He'd settle for six inches and lots of know-how.) But the longer Brent looked up into the stars and let his mind roam, the more persistently these thoughts oppressed him.

He tried to ignore it. He made himself think about jobhunting and the troubles in the Middle East. Puppy dogs and little girls.

But sex was everywhere in the night. The fecund smell of soil. The sheen of sweat. Things rustling and copulating in the bushes and flowers at full bloom.

And Nick. Nick was everywhere. It was as if Nick was outlined in the night sky above him, in a constellation of the brightest stars. Nick was the man he wanted to spend this moment with. The man he saw himself spending this night with.

How ridiculous! Brent thought. He hardly knew the guy! And, more important, what he knew of him was all bad. The guy was a closet case, an asshole, a pretender.

Why, Brent thought, was he always in such a rush to find a new Mr. Right? And why did he keep looking in all the wrong places.

Be patient! he told himself. *Play the field.* Don't obsess about Nick because he happens to be the first halfway-decent looking man you've met since breaking up.

You just got free, enjoy it while it lasts!

He tried to dismiss the thought of Nick as just the product of an idle mind, lost in the countryside, missing the city's tumult and drama.

In his mind, Brent imagined the firmness of those pecs and flat belly. The sweaty writhe of his shoulder muscles under Brent's palms. He imagined digging deep into the flesh with his fingers. Kissing those closed blue eyes with their long lashes. Putting his face in that crotch and...

Suddenly the night was jungle hot and moist, and Brent's hand was in his own pants. He touched himself and imagined it was Nick's touch. Unbuckled his trousers and felt the kiss of the night air. Pulled his cock from his pants. Stroked from the head to the hilt. Weighed his balls in his other hand.

He shifted his weight lower in the chair. Sunken, hidden, eyes closed, he began to jerk himself off.

He imagined himself astride Nick's chest. Rutting against his firm pecs, between them against the sternum. Imagined sliding upward toward Nick's face. Nick taking him in his mouth.

Brent imagined his hands at the back of stone's head, cradling him there. And then, unable to stop himself, unable to resist the stone's hungry tongue, fucking stone's mouth. Fucking it hard, seeing himself, the smaller man, fucking that mouth hard, feeling the slight gag of his tonsils, the danger of teeth, the roughness of tongue.

Brent could feel it now, rising up in him, in his crotch, days' worth of sexlessness, swelling inside him, a tingling in the spine, felt the pressure of his hand on his cock, the tapping of his hand on the downstroke on his balls, and then it all surged up and he convulsed in his chair, and bursts of hot cum shot in the air, landing hot and wet on his belly, leaking around his hand, and he cried out, unable to help himself.

Afterward, he sat, breathing hard, angry with himself as soon as the cum had got cold.

Get a grip, captain. You are not thirteen years old.

***

In the morning after the wedding, the house seemed empty and large. His sisters had all returned to their families. Adam had resumed his summer routine with his rural hiphop friends and work at the tampon factory, which was the only place in the County a kid could get a decent job. Brent wandered dejectedly from room to room, examining the signs of their past.

Brent put himself through his workout of stretching and

exercises and dumbbells. He was not at his peak dancing shape, but he judged the workout not bad for someone who had been bed-ridden after knee surgery for six months. The mirror was kind: he looked good. Muscled. Lean. His skin clear and young looking. He could still pass for twenty, he thought. If he really wanted.

In late morning, Brent and Mrs. Sawyer took coffee together out on the porch. They gossiped about his sisters and the wedding and Heidi's honeymoon in Bermuda. She and Gar had decided sensibly to put it off until the fall, when prices were cheaper. Both of them had already agreed to return to work the very next day.

"I don't understand it," his mother said.

"Well, Ma, it's not like he just deflowered her last night. They know what it's like. It wasn't like when you and Dad were young…."

"Brent!" she scolded.

"Heidi's hardly a virgin, Mom."

Mrs. Sawyer seemed genuinely crushed to hear this fact stated so baldly.

"Well," she said, "I don't think it's right to talk about your own sister that way."

Mrs. Sawyer mentioned old friends of Brent's in Holmstead County—girls, mostly, of course—who had gotten pregnant or married or killed, or had abandoned their children, or gone on to be hookers or drug addicts or Supreme Court justices, or whatever. Mrs. Sawyer had all the scoops on everyone who had ever lived in Holmstead County and she was not afraid to share them.

Brent dutifully asked all the right questions, prompting the reminisces. He enjoyed talking to his mother, and she enjoyed talking to him. It did not matter what they said; they had always been satisfied with one another's company.

Of course, he thought, it's all a game. We both know it. It was all prelude to her asking when he, too, was going to move back from the city, back to the County, so she could have all her children under her wings. Sooner or later, she would make her argument.

Sure enough, she brought up the topic in the next breath. His mother just could not quite understand why he had left, and why he would not ever come back. Ever. No matter what. To her, the best life a person could live was in Holmstead County, and she would always believe it, no matter how many fabulous sights in the City Brent showed her when she came down to visit.

"Mom, don't be greedy...isn't it enough that you've got your four daughters all within an hour's drive?"

"But I want my boys to come home, too," she complained. "I'm your mother. I am *allowed* to be greedy."

At that moment, Adam slumped through the front door on to the porch, grumpy and hungover, eyes at half-mast. He was half-dressed, in a pair of flannel pants, a shirt wrung in his hand, a smudge of dirt on his face.

A horn sounded in the driveway. One of his friends was revving the engine of a souped-up Monte Carlo. The pounding of rap music could be felt as well as heard. Adam again burst out the door, shirt again slung over his shoulder, a box of Cheetos in his hand, and his mouth full. He ran out to the car and jumped in. The Monte Carlo sped off with a scatter of gravel and the squeal of tires when it hit the highway.

Brent laughed. "Be careful what you wish for. Not all your boys are such a joy to have at home."

Mother rolled her eyes.

"Adam's a good boy," she said.

"Of course he is, Ma. He's the best."

Mrs. Sawyer looked back at him gratefully. "You think?"

"Second best boy you ever raised." He placed his hand over his heart.

"Brent Sawyer!"

"I'm kidding, Mom."

After lunch, Brent walked down the back pasture to the river, where he used to swim nude. He took off his shoes and let his toes dangle in the shadowed water. From there, he wandered through the woods to the old abandoned stone railway station at the edge of town. When he was just fifteen, he had conned one of his faghags into taking all kinds of improper brooding pictures of himself naked among the station's stones and pillars.

What a tramp people must have thought I was, getting naked at every opportunity before I had even fully gone through puberty. He remembered how proud he had been of those pictures, because they were objective evidence that he was attractive, more attractive than he had even dared believe at the time.

Next to the station, Brent stretched out in the grass, taking his shirt off and basking in the sun. He dozed fitfully for a few hours. His dreams all involved Nick in various states of undress in the shadows of the railway station.

When Brent woke, again disgusted by the way his thoughts and dreams were betraying him, the sky had darkened overhead. There was a coolness in the air like mint and shade.

The clouds came on suddenly, big black festering things from the Northeast, the color of bruises. The wind whipped the trees and turned up the pale undersides of the leaves. A pair of geese streaked overhead, heading for the shelter of their nest in Sabbaday Lake.

Brent glanced at his watch. He would be lucky to get home before it rained.

Brent took the shortcut home, along the old bridle path. This route brought him to the Old Lady Blanche House. Although he was mindful of the coming rain, Brent could not help but stop. The Lady Blanche House was one of his favorite spots in the whole County. It a mid-nineteenth century mansion that had been let go to ruin.

In his youth, all the windows had been boarded up and "keep out" signs hung on the doors. Brent used to break into it and wander through the faded splendor. The fireplace no longer smelled of ash but only the animal and bird droppings from above. The floorboards had been loose and cranky.

Brent's friends had scared themselves into believing it was haunted, but Brent had always imagined what it was like to have been the lonely widow, Lady Blanche. He had always imagined her dressed in a fine white gown every night, lighting her lanterns until they burned out, waiting for her dead husband to come home.

Now, though, Brent saw that the Lady Blanche house was being restored. The boarded windows had been replaced. A giant stone patio had been added where the wooden deck had once been. A stone chimney was in progress on one side, blending perfectly with the old fieldstone foundation.

Brent was both jealous and grateful. Though he had never given the Lady Blanche house a thought while living in New York City, he had always regarded it as his own. Still, he was pleased that someone was giving it the love it deserved after such a long wait. That was a hopeful sign, he thought. There's hope for us all.

As he admired the work that had been done, the rain began to fall. Big thick drops, large as pearls, began to pelt Brent's hair. He was still a good fifteen minutes' walk from his mother's house; he would be sopped by the time he got there, his hair in ruins!

He looked around him. There were no cars leading up the road to the Lady Blanche house and not a light inside.

What the hell, he thought. It's not like I'm a complete stranger.

He sprinted up to the Lady Blanche House and began to pull on windows and boards and doors until he found a sheet of plywood that was loose.

He yanked hard, and it broke with a snap.

Brent found himself in the parlor room that he had always pictured as a library when he was young. Sure enough, the walls were lined from head to toe with fresh cherry-wood bookcases.

Whoever was restoring the place thinks just like I do! Brent thought. *And he or she has damn good taste.*

Brent went on to the next room, which was dark and gloomy. The only light came through a pair of sliding doors to the patio, which were sheeted in plastic. When his eyes grew accustomed to the dark, Brent could see that whoever was restoring the house was doing a first class job. Even without furnishings, it was appointed with taste: built in bookshelves and window seats; a small cocktail bar; ceilings as high as a chapel; and a giant stone hearth that filled one side of the room. Even the moldings had been lovingly reconstructed.

Some rich homo must be doing this work, Brent thought. *No one in Holmstead County would ever build something so beautiful. Their idea of nice housing was a brand new double wide.*

Because the storm outside showed no sign of abating, Brent snooped around into some of the other rooms. They were even darker than the rest of the house, and the walls were unfinished. Electric wires dangled, unconnected, and even the floorboards underfoot were suspect.

It would take a while, Brent reflected, to repair thirty years of neglect.

Brent was still feeling his way through the narrow Victorian servants' hallways when suddenly the whole house was flooded with light. Brent was blinded by the sudden brightness and staggered against the wall. He heard from the front room the sound of heavy footsteps.

Instinctively, Brent ducked into a side hall, and he had hardly gone two steps when the plywood floorboard gave way beneath his foot. His leg plunged in up to the ankle, and he was thrown forward to his face.

As he fell, Brent waited for his knee to give that too-familiar sickening pop. He braced the white-hot pain.

Miraculously, the joint held out. He lay there a moment, face down on the floorboards, scarcely believing he had not again injured himself. He had been lucky not to have fucked up his knee all over again. Three months more in bed.

Again, he heard the footsteps, and Brent pushed himself to his feet. He reached down two hands and struggled to free his ankle, which was caught in the splintered floorboard as firmly as if it were a jaw.

But Brent could get no leverage to yank it out. The harder he pushed on the plywood with his other foot, the more the rest of the plywood threatened to give way. He glanced down the hall, then back at his ankle. The footsteps were getting closer.

Desperately, he yanked once more. Then looked up at the string of bare bulbs hanging like Christmas decorations over the beams. *Maybe he could yank the string down and smash them and he would not get caught!*

A shadow fell over him, and he looked up, guilty and cowering before the unhappy homeowner. With a light at his back, making him look as if he had a halo or aura, Nick looked like an angry God.

"You!" Nick spluttered.

"Me," Brent agreed weakly.

"What in God's name are you doing here?"

"I was trying to get out of the rain."

"Do you typically break into people's houses to escape the rain?"

"Well, no, I was just...this house used to be...one of my favorites, I was just curious.... Look, why don't you make yourself useful and help me get out of here?"

Obediently, Nick stepped forward carefully bracing himself on the beams between which the plywood stretched so that he did not break it.

"Plywood's not supposed to hold you up," he pointed out. "Even someone as light on his feet as you."

Brent was not sure whether the comment was an insult or a compliment, but for the moment he was more concerned about breaking free. Nick seized his ankle.

His hands were hard and strong. Brent felt the calloused fingers against his skin.

Nick yanked so hard that Brent lost his balance, and he had to snatch at Nick's bent back for balance. The muscles were hard, solid defined. He felt as if he could have found a handhold under the bulge of his lats or traps. It was like an instant anatomy lesson.

Brent clung to Nick for a precarious moment, as close to him as a second skin. His mind filled with the prior night's fantasy and the day's dreams, and he blushed crimson, as if Nick could read his mind.

A thunderclap shook the house.

Brent released his hold on Nick. "That was a close one," he said.

Nick did not release his ankle. His fingers stroked the bare skin just above his sock. This quick movement from strength to gentleness stirred something deep in Brent. For a moment, he felt a sadness he did not even know he possessed, something deep inside himself that was as vulnerable as a child.

"What are you doing?"

"No cuts, a little abrasion, no more," Nick pronounced. He released the ankle and Brent was instantly sorry he had done so. He would have obediently and gladly stood for hours feeling those fingers encircle his limbs.

Nick's eyes moved over Brent's body as if he planned to eat him and he was looking for the right place to dig in. The force of his look was palpable. Brent had rarely been frisked as intrusively, even at an airport.

Nick leaned slightly closer and it felt like a wall was toppling over. Nick sniffed the air, as if he was testing Brent's scent.

"I love the smell of rain in the spring," he said. His voice was husky and full of throat.

"It's summer."

Again, Brent felt that chill of quick fear. Nick was standing too close. Although he had released Brent's ankle, Brent still felt as if he was firmly within Nick's grip. In his complete control.

No one would hear me if I screamed, he thought. There was nothing around the Lady Blanche House for a mile. Nothing but forest, and the rarely traveled bridle path, and the wash of heavy rain.

This huge hulking stud could break me open, if that was what he wanted, Brent thought. And Brent had been around enough horny men in his lifetime to know that was what Nick wanted. Wanted in the worst way.

"Are you all right?" Nick asked.

"Fine, fine, fine." Brent backed away from him, each step feeling as if Nick's grip had relaxed. *Fear is such an odd thing,* Brent thought. *What is it I am afraid of?*

"You look pale," Nick said. The tone of his voice did not show concern. Rather, Nick was studying Brent with his head cocked, as if he were something curious at the end of a microscope, the way a scientist might regard a bug, some lesser form on the food chain.

Nick turned on his heel.

"Come into the kitchen," he invited, "It's the only place that's anywhere near finished."

The kitchen was a warm open room, with terra cotta tiles and stainless-steel appliances and a breakfast bar. Even in the darkness of the storm, it looked as if it were lit by a dozen suns.

Nick said, "Combination of skylights and coloring. Shades of the Mediterranean."

"You're a mind reader!"

"Nah—it's the first thing everyone notices, is the light." He paused a moment and then added, "I designed it myself."

"Nice work."

Nick poured him a glass of water. Brent was about to take it when Nick suddenly hedged.

"Why don't you take off your shirt?" Nick suggested.

As soon as the words were out of his mouth, Nick blushed a fiery intense red that climbed up from his collar and turned his face nearly purple. He hemmed and hawed, and coughed, but could not seem to find what he had meant to say.

Brent raised his eyebrows. Perhaps he was not the only one with guilty fantasies?

Nick added, weakly, "I mean, we'll hang it to dry." He turned away, rummaged in one of the closets. "I've got a fan here somewhere, that ought to blow it dry."

To Brent, it looked like Nick was relieved to find a place to hide. For a moment, he was still. When he turned, he had a tiny oscillating fan in his hand that was the size of a grapefruit.

He looked Brent frankly in the eye. Nick's transformation from trembles to firmness was complete.

"Sorry, the dryer's not hooked up yet."

Brent was amused by Nick's internal struggle. He had not run across a man so careful of his own desire in years. He thought: *But how close it all is to the surface. This man's heart. This man's desire. You would think from years of trying to bottle it up, he would be out of touch with it all.*

The realization was a flash of lightning, and he felt suddenly like he understood everything. With a sudden burst of inspiration, Brent peeled his wet shirt off over his head. Then, for good measure, he pulled off his pants as well. He stood proudly in the bikini underwear he had forgotten he had put on that morning.

Nick had turned to plug in the fan, but the wet slap of clothes caused him to look back. His eyes bulged. He swallowed hard.

Brent thought: *This guy's heart is available to me, like a fruit on a low-hanging branch.*

Brent did not blush or retreat. He tried to catch Nick's gaze, but Nick's eyes were elsewhere, jumpy, alive, exploring Brent's body. Brent did not mind. He was a performer, used to the stage, to carrying the weight of hungry eyes, to old queens who came again and again to the same show just to see him. To see his body. To enjoy it. Brent took pleasure in their satisfaction. He always had.

He held out his clothes expectantly so that Nick had to come to him to fetch them. For a moment, it looked as if Nick might refuse to come forward for the wet clothing. Riveted, hard as marble, but visibly trembling, vibrating like a tuning fork.

Brent turned slightly, tightening the muscles of his abdomen. He had been dancing for years. He knew exactly what he looked like. Exactly the right angle of torsion that would put his body at its best. Its most inviting.

When Nick finally moved, the three steps forward were dream-steps, leaden and reluctant. He did not meet Brent's gaze when he took the clothes. His eyes were busy on the angles and fruits of Brent's body. His gaze was a pair of high-voltage klieg lights, burning, searing his skin.

In a moment or two, he had succeeded in making Brent feel as raw and naked as he ever had. As if Nick would know everything about him, seeing it all effortlessly, right through the skin.

The secrets of Brent's soul were not necessarily things he wanted Nick to be reading at that moment. They were quite X-rated. Brent almost regretted that Nick had not taken advantage of him while he was trapped in the plywood. Forcing him while his leg was cuffed and he could not get away. Could not say no. Now *that* would have been kind of hot.

He crouched to shield the exposed parts of his body from Nick's acetylene stare. He used his ankle for an excuse, rubbing it ruefully. He was glad at the chance to look away from Nick's looking at him.

When Nick spoke, his voice came as a surprise. Gentle and concerned. Not as rough as Brent remembered it.

Or, maybe not as rough as I wanted it, Brent thought.

"Are you sure your leg is all right? Heidi told me..." Nick broke off as if he had spoken too much.

Brent finished his sentence for him: "Heidi told you that I destroyed my career in a drunken fall from a two-foot-high box in the middle of a dance floor at a gay club? Is that what you were going to say?"

"I didn't know it happened that way."

"Yeah, well. Not the way I expected to go out either. But shit happens, right?"

Nick winced at the curse, but said nothing. For some reason, his disapproval touched Brent. It seemed so old-fashioned. So quaint.

My God, he thought, *if he disapproves of me now for letting loose with an S-bomb, just think if he saw the real me down in the city at one of the bars. This guy is a piece of work. A unicorn.*

"It's no problem," he assured Nick, speaking rapidly, to brush

47

away the curse. "I'm at peace with it. Not going to cry over it. What's done is done."

Nick nodded. He said nothing. It was as if he did not believe Brent. And Brent suddenly felt like he *needed* Nick to believe him. Nick above all others.

"Really," he insisted. "It would have happened anyway, the doctors said. Sooner or later. The joint was weak."

Brent heard his own voice. It sounded like he was making an excuse for himself. Which made him color. He did not want anyone to think he didn't take responsibility for what had happened. Or that he was whining. He meant it when he said he was at peace. For reasons he dared not even examine, he did not want Nick of all people to doubt him on this score.

Anyone else, any other issue. But not on this point. Not with Nick.

The moment broke and Nick moved deliberately and abruptly around the kitchen. He stretched Brent's pants and shirt carefully across a pair of unfinished beams so they would not wrinkle.

Brent was again touched by this extra bit of care. Why on earth would the man care if his clothes were wrinkled? Nick's own were dirty and sweat-stained.

"I heard you were a very accomplished dancer," Nick said. His eyes were on the clothing's gentle movement, rapt as someone who appreciated symphony.

"Not bad."

"I think I saw you in La Traviata."

Brent was startled. "La Traviata at the Kaufmann Center?"

"Yes. Exactly. Two years ago. December 17," he said precisely. Brent guessed that Nick always employed mathematical precision. He would know the names of everything and keep careful tally of dates. For all his brutal strength, he was a man of detail.

"I was down in the City for an installation at the OSP Gallery," Nick said. "And we decided to take in a show."

Never in a million years would he have pictured this brooding, beautiful hulk choosing to attend a modern dance in the city. Let alone at the OSP. A tractor pull, maybe.

"Don't act so surprised," Nick said. "It's not very flattering."

"I didn't know you required flattery."

"Touché."

Nick turned and leaned back against the counter. He was again observing Brent critically.

"You're very agile," Nick said.

"Don't act so surprised..."

"I can see why you made a good dancer," Nick continued without letting Brent finish, as if the observation, repeating Nick's own, were not worth making. Or hearing. Or paying any attention to whatsoever. "You'd make a nice bantamweight fighter as well. You've got the bod-...the frame for it. Like Hector...who was that bantam weight a few years back?"

Brent did not know or care a whit about boxing. But it intrigued him that this man who had attended La Traviata would also be knowledgeable about such a brutal sport.

They looked at one another frankly. Mutually appreciative.

Even though they were ten feet apart, Brent had the sinking feeling they were standing much too close together. For anyone's good.

And yet he could not...and would not...drop Nick's gaze. Not this time. It felt too much like a challenge, a test. A fight to the death. Nick was trying to bully him, he felt sure of it. Brent felt sure Nick often got away with bullying people because of his size and his beauty.

When Nick terminated the staring contest, Brent felt a brief flush of triumph. He was pleased with himself. He had won round one. He looked down at his body. Half-naked, no less.

Nick waved his huge hand to encompass the room. "What do you think of my kitchen?" he asked.

"It's beautiful," Brent said truthfully. "Really. It looks like you're hoping to have a professional cook."

"I am a professional cook. Or I was. I don't like second-rate kitchens."

"I'll bet you don't like second-rate anything."

Nick tested him with his eyes, but apparently decided Brent was not mocking him. Brent was not so sure. His flirting came to him without effort or thought, part mocking, part flattery, and he rarely knew how much of either. In this way, he, too, was a bit of a chef, tossing a word salad.

"I only take the best." For some reason, the words sounded to Brent like a gentle put-down. As if he should not be disappointed should Nick not choose him.

"Me, too," Brent said, belligerently.

Nick said abruptly, "I'm behind schedule."

"Well, don't wait for me, I can walk home."

"No, no," Nick said, too fast, as if he did not want Brent to leave. "I mean, on the kitchen."

Nick dusted some sawdust off the counter and tinkered with a lazy Susan that he seemed to think was not properly spinning. He saw a hundred flaws that Brent could not see.

"Looks fine to me."

"No, trust me, there's lots of work. I want it to be perfect. We're going to move in here after we're married."

Brent's response was automatic and unthinking: "Yeah, *whatever.*"

Nick's face flushed, as bruised as the storm clouds had been before the rain broke. His knuckles turned white where they gripped the counter. Then, as quickly as it had come over him, his body relaxed. He breathed out a long slow breath, hands clenched and unclenched. His face was expressionless.

"Someone like you would never understand," he said.

"Are you still in the closet? Is that it?" Brent tried to keep the scorn out of his voice. He had spent only about two weeks in the closet when he was fifteen years old, but he knew it was harder for some people. Perhaps especially people like Nick, whom everyone expected to be a 'real man.'

Nick chewed his thick lower lip as he thought through his answer. Finally, he said, "My situation is more complex than the simple terms you'd like to describe it in."

"Well, come on...I mean, either you're in the closet or you're out. There's no halfway."

"You don't understand...."

"You are! You're a big freakin' closet case, aren't you?"

Nick denied it.

"Or...it's don't ask, don't tell, is that it? I mean, my sister doesn't even know."

"Of course, your sister knows. But I'm pleased that she can keep a secret. Which is more, frankly, than I would ever put past her brother!"

This information took Brent aback. How dare his sister keep this dish from him. He was family. He had a right to know.

"What you don't understand," Nick said, "is the concept of discretion. The better part of valor, remember?"

"But it's dishonest."

"It's nothing of the kind," he said with business-like certainty and efficiency. He acted as if that was the end of the road, an incontrovertible argument. This annoying habit of dismissing all doubts, as if he had long considered them before, made Brent feel slow and stupid. And unable to keep his mouth shut.

"You should tell *her*, at least."

"Who?"

"Your bride."

"My bride is well aware of my situation," Nick said haughtily.

Again, the news, if true, was stunning. There was more to this puzzle than Brent had guessed. Or at least involved more conspirators than he had imagined.

"And she still wants to marry you?"

"Yes. Believe it or not, she finds plenty in me that's worth marrying."

"No doubt. Like U.S. citizenship!"

"You're hopelessly simple. You just cannot conceive that two people might unite out of things other than base instincts. Do the words honor, commitment, family, etc., mean nothing to you?"

"They mean everything to me. And that's why I find what you .. you people are doing...despicable."

"She's a very bright girl. Very serious. She'll be getting her PhD soon," he added proudly, "and her with two children!"

"She's using you."

"No, Una and I understand one another."

Outside, the rain had not abated. It was drenching the kitchen skylight, like a patter of war drums. Nick looked surprisingly eager to convince Brent on this point. His eyes were searching Brent's face as if he might read there the questions and anticipate every doubt.

"Look," he said, "if I were to advertise my sexuality, that would jeopardize our chances of demonstrating this is a legitimate marriage to the INS. One need not broadcast every bit of detail about one's personal life. I have no obligation to do so at all."

"But it's *not* a legitimate marriage!"

"It is," Nick repeated firmly. His will was irrevocable, his determination like stone. Which, under other circumstances, Brent might have found admirable. But which he could not accept in one so deeply wrong.

Nick held up a hand like a stop sign. "It is a legitimate marriage, I told you that. It's just not a marriage that's based on sex. We have a certain deeper...sympathy for one another. Which is what you don't seem to be able to understand."

Brent could not abide any longer this combination of appealing romanticism and stubborn superiority with which Nick spoke. There was nothing that got him so worked up as someone who thought he had all the answers.

"Sit down," Brent commanded. He directed Nick to the breakfast nook. They each took one of the Parisian stools. All he needed were Gauloises and demitasse, Brent thought irreverently. Which would look silly in Nick's giant hands.

And speaking of silly, a voice inside Brent said, *would you take*

a look at yourself running around in this half-constructed kitchen in your
underwear? No wonder he doesn't take you seriously.

"Don't you tell me what I can and cannot understand, Nick. I understand plenty. If you were sixty years old I might—maybe—be able to understand a marriage of that kind. And only just maybe. But you cannot deny biology. You're, what?.... thirty years old? No way you can pretend that sex is not a driving factor. I'm just being realistic. You should be, too."

"There are higher functions than sex. And higher commands to control the baser impulses. Biology is not a god."

Their legs brushed against one another under the table, and they both pulled them apart as if from electric shock. Nick's touch on Brent's bare ankle almost made him leap out of his skin.

Nick looked flustered. Brent felt lobotomized. All the good arguments had been obliterated from his head by that one touch.

He spluttered and vented and cursed himself and brushed a hand over his chest as if he could clothe it with magic. Finally Brent got out, "Even if I concede that point—and I think it's bullshit, by the way—any relationship that doesn't account for sex and romance is doomed to failure. But imagining you guys are above all that as you seem to think—there's more than just the pair of you to think about, isn't there."

At the mention of others in the equation, Nick—who seemed to have been mesmerized by Brent's hand running over his own bare chest—woke up. He crossed his arms in front of his chest.

Brent noticed his pecs were like a cleavage. His forearms were powerful ropes, knotted and twined like a jungle vine. His jaw set with the ferocious tenacity of a bulldog, which only added a brutal strength to his Grecian, handsome face.

What a face! It was animated and bronzed; the skin was clear and good, but not too smooth. The only wrinkle showed at the corners of the eye, and then just made him look wise and hardened.

Brent was again distracted. He had to shake his head clear of visions of stroking those high cheekbones and the spread of stubble on the chin before he could again climb aboard his train of thought.

"What do you mean?" Nick growled. It seemed like days later. Brent could not even remember what they had been talking about.

"What?"

"What do you mean I have obligations to others?"

"Wha—Oh. I mean, people who have known you as gay will think you—we—can 'change.' It lends credence to all those gay-reprogramming things fundamentalists try to urge on us. What do you do about that?"

"Who is 'we'?"

"We is gay people. Homosexuals. We is you," Brent said pointedly.

"My obligation is only to myself. I am not responsible—nor do I care—what people think." Nick looked thrilled to have the chance to disavow the importance of other people's opinions.

Brent barely concealed a smile, because he too had felt the influence of that drug at some point in his life—the undeniable attraction of seeing oneself as alone on an island. The problem was, it was not true.

"And then there's the political meaning of marrying," he pointed out. "I mean, it's an institution denied to the rest of gay men. And you are going to participate in it, support it?"

"It takes more than a law to form a marriage. As far as I'm concerned, most gay men aren't capable of the kind of commitment a marriage requires, anyhow."

"Oh, boohoo, that sounds like the ranting of some right-wing kook. I—"

"In my case, it's the product of personal experience."

"Get a life. Don't blame one—"

Nick moved so suddenly that the words were still coming out of Brent's mouth when Nick's lips closed firmly over his. His tongue parted Brent's lips, and his hand slipped behind his neck, freezing Brent, holding him cocked and ready.

Brent felt like a butterfly in a collection, stuck through with pins, stuck firmly in place. He could not help but respond to the brutal kiss.

Nick's breath was hot and sweet. The lips firm, the tongue animal, raspy, probing. The smell of his skin was masculine and intoxicating, somehow richer than Brent had even imagined it would be, with the slightest taste of clean over it all.

It was like a tidal wave closing over his head. Fighting for the surface before he drowned, flailing. He felt his cock go hard in his underwear and was unable to mask it.

If Nick's hands go any lower on my body, Brent thought, *I'll be lost.*

He would immediately surrender. And for a moment, he wanted nothing more than to feel that large hand on his neck descend over his bare torso, brushing his rock-hard nipples. Down along his ribs, to his butt and hip and pelvis. In his crotch. Around his cock, under his balls, weighing, teasing, fingering his asshole in a slow agonizing circle.

Brent suddenly found his strength. He shoved Nick away. It was a little like trying to push over a brick wall. He succeeded mainly in flattening himself against the wall of the breakfast nook with Nick still poised halfway over the table, mid-kiss.

Brent's breath was coming in great big rasps, and his cock was painfully hard beneath his bikini briefs, straining against the material. Every muscle was taut as piano wire. Brent touched himself, smoothed himself down, and then dared steal a look at Nick.

Brent had expected Nick to look pleased with himself. Triumphant. *Look at the rise he got out of me,* Brent thought, *who wouldn't be triumphant?*

But Nick looked furious, as if Brent was to blame for the kiss. For Nick's tongue in Brent's mouth. For the war in the Middle East and the popularity of chartreuse and cruelty to puppies and every other wrong in the world.

"What?" Nick snarled. "Stop looking at me like that. Isn't that what you wanted?"

Brent was still trying to catch his breath. The kiss had been like a punch in the stomach. His mouth felt used. Bruised. He patted himself down for a tube of chapstick and realized he was still in his underwear. He closed his arms around his chest.

"Nothing. I'm...I...just..."

Nick snorted with disgust. A fierce, dragon-like sound that conveyed all the disdain in the world.

The weak feeling in Brent turned to anger.

"What *I* wanted? Is that what you said, Mr. Tongue-Down-the-Throat?!" he shrieked. "What I wanted?!" Brent was acutely aware of the high pitch and volume of his voice. It reverberated around the stones of the kitchen and would have broken glass had Nick yet purchased any stemware.

Brent accused, "You were the one who kissed me, remember? You—the 'straight' married man. What *I* wanted. Yeah, right!"

Brent stewed for several more minutes about the absurdity of the idea. But in truth, he had wanted it. He had wanted it since the first time he had met Nick, and the continuing hardness between his legs was the proof of it.

He dropped his hands down to form a fig leaf around his member. Lord knows, it would not be the first time his cock betrayed him. But this time he was struck to the quick. He was ashamed. Ashamed of the animal feelings that had allowed this kiss to happen and him to respond to it. To want it. Even now to want it again. To be hopeful that Nick would tell him to shut up, and seize him, and force himself on him. To scare him, to know him, to own and obliterate him. No apologies, no regrets.

"Are you quite finished?" Nick asked. His tone was withering and cold. It seemed impossible that a man that had just fired Brent with that molten kiss could possibly be so chilly.

"'Quite?' 'Quite?'" Brent heard himself ask. "What, are you channeling your grandmother?"

Nick grunted and wrestled himself out of the nook, nearly upending the table between them in the process. He took one step away, and then whirled on Brent. He spoke from close range, where his mouth seemed big, his teeth white, his face purple with anger, flecks of spit like bullets in the bright light of his fancy designer kitchen.

"Oh, come on, don't play innocent with me, Brent Sawyer!"

It was the first time Nick had used his full name, and the beauty of it on his lips startled Brent. "Look," he said, "I didn't ask for—"

"You come to my house, you look at me that way you have, you undress me with your eyes, you wear that white shirt, you drag me over to this table, you flaunt that cock"—here he dashed all Brent's hopes that Nick had not witnessed the erection—"and put your face right in mine, and then you pretend to be surprised when I kiss you?!"

Brent opened his mouth to argue, but Nick was backing away now, dismissing him, wagging his finger in front of him like a scold. Like he could cancel Brent out. Or obliterate him.

"I get it now," Nick said. "You're one of those teases, are you? Never live up to the promises your body makes. I should have known it, just from the look of you. This reckless, inconsiderate, wimpy, dishonest, game-playing cocktease, that's all you are."

He waved at Brent's body without the least shred of respect. And then, as if even permitting himself a reference to that forbidden body was too much, Nick sprang closer toward him.

Again, Brent felt a trace of fear. He did not know this guy from Adam. And Nick was big. Much, much bigger than Brent. Dangerously big. He remembered how fast Nick had moved, like a bolt of lightning.

Brent, too, slipped away from the table. He danced out of reach. But it was not in Brent's nature to shut up. Screw the danger. He had too much pride to let this guy—or any guy—get away with disrespecting him.

"I'm no tease. And who says I'm even interested? Yesterday, maybe, but that was before I learned what a complete, right-wing, ass-backward, chickenshit closet case you are."

Brent let loose a string of insults. His fury had reached a new pitch. He was now furious, not only at everything Nick had said, but that Nick had managed to physically frighten him on top of it all.

But when he paused for breath, Nick was undamaged. Unmoved. He had not retreated a step. He said quietly, "You're a tease and you know it. You're all teases. Every single one of you."

For a moment the words hung in the air between them. And then Nick stormed from the kitchen, and the words seemed to crash to the ground. Brent, startled, blinked once, twice. *All of who are teases? Men? Gays? Everybody?*

The childish accusation seemed like a crack in Nick's stone face. In his veneer. And Brent felt the tenderness he might feel not toward a lover but toward a child.

He listened to Nick's steady footsteps on the unfinished floors, like the stomps of a petulant adolescent. Echoing in the empty house. The lonely house.

He gave chase. Snatching at his arm, Brent attempted to whirl Nick around to face him. To face reality.

The result was as if he brought a wall of stones tumbling down on himself. An avalanche of flesh.

Again, Nick seized Brent. For the briefest second, he gripped him, held him, visibly vibrating with some internal conflict Brent could not fathom. Now that he had Brent in his mitts again, Nick seemed not to know what to do with him.

And then, Nick pressed him to the wall and again kissed him. Hard. Good. Forcing his body against Brent's. Rubbing. Crushing him with its size and power. His lips fit over Brent with an air-tight seal. Brent could feel the hard cock through Nick's pants. He felt as if he would have felt it through a brick wall. Hard. Insistent. Demanding.

He felt a weakness in his belly, a quiver of his sphincter, the sproinging of his own member.

The kiss and the cock took all the fire from Brent's fury. His legs went weak and rubbery, as they had with white-hot pain the night his knee had collapsed. The air seemed to be changing colors between them.

When they parted, they were panting. Faces inches from one another. Eyes moving back and forth, probing one another, getting ready for another plunge.

Brent murmured, "I don't think this is such a good idea." He was dizzy, not sure if it was lingering from the kiss, or something else entirely. He felt delirious. He did not know what he was saying. Or thinking.

He drew back an inch. Maybe two. He searched Nick's face— saw nothing there. No relief. No kindness. Nothing human.

It was just a black hole. Pure matter. Whose gravity was pulling him away from himself. He stifled a spasm, an urge to give himself entirely to this powerful force. To submit. To be obliterated and used and maybe even discarded, he just did not care, not now.

With a superhuman effort, Brent tore himself away. He ducked beneath Nick's outstretched arms and retreated to the window. He stood there for what seemed like ages. Clutching himself. Seeing nothing. He might as well have been standing facing a blank wall.

Finally, he managed to say, "Look, I think maybe it's beginning to clear up."

It was an idiotic comment. Inane and silly. And it rang in the kitchen like a cheap tin whistle. Brent immediately wished he had not said it. That some greater, intelligent, witty phrase might have come to mind and been served up. Something he could be proud of. Something that would win a laugh.

The storm was nowhere near spent. It was forbidding and dangerous, and the wind resolutely howled over the open meadows as if it were the dark of winter.

Nick's stillness was unbearable. It was all Brent could do to keep himself from turning. From looking. From knowing what Nick was up to. From asking him what on earth he was thinking. From taking his hand even, and walking him to an open space on the floor where they could make love until the rain stopped.

The first noise, when it came, was the scrape of a boot. As if

Nick had just wiped something unpleasant off his shoe. He marched across the room to the front door, where he stopped. Brent sensed that he was facing the door. Away from Brent. Not looking at his puckered ass beneath the underwear.

He was a statue in the park. An imitation of a once-living man.

This never happened, Brent told himself.

And then he heard Nick turn.

Brent did not turn. He resolutely kept his eyes on the outdoors. On the distance. He did not breathe.

Nick growled, "As soon as the rain stops, I want you out of here, you got it?"

Brent swallowed hard. His tongue was peanut butter in his mouth.

"Thanks for showing me..."

The door slammed as Nick ran out into the storm.

CHAPTER 6

The damp clothes or the unseasonable weather struck Brent with a summer fever. His temperature spiked, his stomach was upset, and it felt as if a pair of coal miners had taken to drilling in his head.

For three days, Brent was laid out with no thought of anything but his own misery. He tossed and turned and sweat until his sheets were wet. He bitched and moaned at his sisters, who dropped by to give their mother a rest and made annoying efforts to cheer him up.

To make matters worse, he tortured himself with thoughts of the abortive encounter with Nick.

Tease! Nick had dared call him a 'tease'?! It was Nick who had stolen the kiss, not Brent! Nick who had been the cause of this whole problem. It was infuriating that he would try to turn the tables and pin the blame on Brent!

But some part of Brent suspected the accusation was right on. What force had brought him to that house of all places? He could have walked to town. He could have remained in the shelter of the old railway station. And why hadn't he guessed when he saw the fine stone work on the Lady Blanche House that it was Nick's handiwork? In retrospect, it was obvious. So obvious that, deep inside, Brent knew he probably *had* guessed, had actually known in the deep recesses of his twisted mind, that it was Nick. And had secretly hoped he would be caught!

The foolishness of the whole situation was beginning to wear on him. It was so juvenile! This, he thought, was what came of playing games with closeted guys. You ended up back in Junior

High School! Brent decided that he would go back to the city as soon as he was well again.

And then another spiking fever laid him low, and he thought: maybe I'll just die here quietly instead.

On the fourth day Brent felt well enough to sit up. To get a moment alone, he encouraged his mother to go into town for groceries—and assured her she did not have to summon one of his sisters to baby-sit.

The solitude was pleasing. He spread a blanket on the floor and began to put his body into a few easy positions. It was the first time he had done a workout in days and his joints were tight and unforgiving. Gently, he stretched and eased them. While he was holding a position, there was no time to think of anything else. He had to concentrate to maintain it, and it kept him in the present.

He had just finished up and put himself back under the blankets when there was a knock on the bedroom door. It was Adam, oddly docile, bearing a glass of orange juice.

"What's up, sport?"

"Nothin'...Mom said to check on you. Make sure you weren't dead." He handed over the OJ and then took a seat at the end of the bed. He was obviously ready to talk. "When are you going to get better?"

"I am better. A little."

"Are you going to go away again once you're better?"

"You sound disappointed, champ...aren't you worried I'll crimp your style?"

"You're the only one who's any fun anymore. Everyone's *married.*"

"Careful, one of these days you'll let one of these girls catch you and you'll be married, too. Happens to the best of them."

"Nah...I'm going to be just like you." Adam colored and shifted uneasily at the end of the bed. "With girls, I mean."

"Don't worry .. it's not catching..." Brent joked, amused by his little brother's shy affection and boyish pride. Suddenly Brent stiffened. He heard an unmistakable male voice in the hallway beneath.

He looked accusingly at Adam.

"What?" Adam said.

"Who the hell is that downstairs?"

"It's this guy that brought Mom home. Her car broke down and he gave her lift. She invited him in." Then a lightbulb flashed on in his head and Adam grinned his big boyish grin. "He's really handsome, Brent," he teased. "You'd love him."

"That shows you how well you know my type, Sporto. I know that guy. I met him at the wedding. We hate each other."

"Really? That's not what he told Mom."

Adam started to get up, but Brent leaned forward in the bed and snatched at his wrist, pinning him down.

"What do you mean? What did he say? Did he say something about me? C'm'ere ya little brat."

Then he released Adam's wrist. "Ah, forget it," Brent said. "Why should I care?"

"Why? Hey, what's up?"

"Nothing."

"You hot for him, dude?"

"He's getting married, wise-ass!"

Adam looked wounded. "I know. I was only kidding. I was just trying to tease you."

Brent nodded. An uneasy silence fell between them.

Brent tried to keep his lips shut. But it was like someone else was in control.

"So...what did he say, Adam?"

"I dunno. Just stuff. So, when are you going back to New York?"

"Soon. Tell me what he said, Champ. I need to know."

Adam shrugged. "He said you two had talked in the rain. Said you had good taste in houses. An' stuff."

Brent was disappointed. This was unsatisfying, tepid stuff. As if he had not affected Nick the way Nick had affected him. He would rather have had Nick attack his character and reputation, even spit on him, rather than this lukewarm treatment, as if he was not even worth getting worked up about.

Brent heaved himself from bed.

"What are you doing?" Adam asked. "Mom said..."

"I'm going to get some respect!"

Brent trooped downstairs swaddled in a quilt.

"Dressed like that?" Adam asked from the top of the stairs.

Nick was sitting in the living room, looking absurdly large in Mrs. Sawyer's Victorian furniture, with a cup of tea balanced on his knee. His legs, Brent noticed, were crossed at the knee.

"Brent-dear, you're awake!" his mother exclaimed.

"Yes," he growled. "Wide-awake."

Nick had a soft smile on his face, as if he were watching a goofy sitcom.

Brent stood in the door to the sitting room, suddenly embarrassed but still defiant. He knew he looked puffy and flushed and far from his best.

Mrs. Sawyer beamed. "I understand you know Nick already," she said.

"Had the pleasure," Brent snapped.

"The car broke down. Luckily, Nick was passing and he called the tow truck and gave me a ride home. Wasn't that nice of him?"

"He's just that kind of guy, I guess."

"I hear you caught something in that rain," Nick said.

"More than I bargained for, that's for sure. I was just looking for a place to get dry. *Nothing* more. What about you?"

"I don't get sick."

"Of course you don't. Not a big strong stud like yourself."

"Well!" Mrs. Sawyer said, looking from one to the other, realizing they were speaking in some sort of code and deciding whether she should try to break in instead of trying to break it.

Brent excused himself to go to the kitchen for some hot tea.

Nick jumped up. "I'll join you," he said. "I could use a refill. And you, Mrs. Sawyer? Can I get you something more?"

"Oh, heavens no. One is plenty for me."

Brent scowled. He led the way to the pantry with Nick hot on his heels. When the kitchen door had shut behind them, Brent demanded, "What are you doing here?"

"I'm getting some tea." Nick said innocently. "Isn't that what you wanted?"

He sized up the kitchen at a glance, finding the kettle and cranking the flame to high.

"You should really leave. Or were you hoping to trap me in a whole series of Holmstead County kitchens for another repressed kiss?"

"I'm sorry about that," Nick said evenly. "I guess we got carried away."

"*You* got carried away."

"*I* got carried away. Sorry."

He did not look sorry. Not sorry enough anyhow.

Brent snapped, "Apologies accepted. Now, there's the door."

"I can't go, Brent. Your mother invited me in. It would be rude. And..."

"No, really...I'll tell her something came up. You had an emergency." Brent again pointed to the door, which caused the quilt to come loose. The glimpse of bare skin made Nick smile.

Brent scowled. He again let the quilt drop, exposing a bare hip, a peek of pubic hair. He drew a line with a wet finger down the crease where his leg joined his torso.

"You like what you see?"

Nick did not immediately respond. His eyes followed Brent's finger as if they were on a string.

"Not bad," Nick choked out. His lips were dry, and it sounded like his tongue was made of parchment. "Now, why don't you button that up before your Mom comes in."

"She's seen it before."

"Honestly...please."

The pot on the stove was beginning to boil, the water roiling furiously and the whistle starting at a low, hollow pitch.

Nick shifted uncomfortably, glanced at the door, swallowed hard, and then looked at Brent again. He made a move, but Brent stepped back and raised his hand in a giant stop sign.

"Ah-ah-ah, Mr. Eager-boy. No touch."

Nick ignored him. He reached to the edge of the quilt and firmly knotted it back into place.

"OK," Brent announced, "you've seen the goods you came to see. Time to go."

"I really can't go, Brent."

The whistle of the pot grew louder, and the steam poured out in a great stream that nearly reached the ceiling. Little flecks of water spit and sizzled on the hot stovetop.

"Sure you can. Just put one foot in front of the other..."

"I can't do that. Trust me. It's not the most comfortable situation for me either, but we both have to learn how to deal."

"Why? What are you talking about?"

Nick shrugged. "It's business. It has nothing to do with you."

"Business?"

"Your mother asked me to do some work around the house..."

Now Brent was furious. He shook his finger at Nick's face. "Oh, no! No way!"

"Way."

"You didn't actually accept, did you?" he asked incredulously.

"I did."

"But - but - but you *can't.*"

"Why can't I? We all have to eat."

"She didn't mean it, you know, she was just being polite, because you gave her a ride home."

"I don't think so."

"Well, whatever." Brent set his arms across his bare chest. "I forbid it." The quilt again slipped. Nick reached out gently, but Brent knocked his hand away and did the job himself.

"Well, no offense," Nick said reasonably, "but I don't think it's your decision, is it?"

Brent felt like he was losing his advantage.

"You'd go to these lengths to pursue me, you sick closet-case?"

Nick pursed his lips, but his voice and manner were as controlled as ever.

"Trust me," Nick said, "I'm not pursuing you. I don't even like you. I couldn't be more pleased if you told me you were leaving tomorrow."

Brent found himself saying—even before he had a chance to think—"Well, I'm not leaving here tomorrow. I'm staying the whole summer."

He spoke defiantly, voice raised above the sound of the kettle. It had become a kind of contest between them to see who would ignore it longest.

Nick shrugged, "Then you better get used to me."

He was smug and confident, and his eyes firmly locked in Brent's.

"You've got some attitude, mister."

"Yeah?"

"Speaking to me in my house..."

"It's not your house. You're not even from here. You'll go back to New York where you and your kind belong, and everybody here will go back to the lives they were living and never think of you again."

"Ahem."

They had been so busy arguing at the top of their lungs that they had not noticed Brent's mother standing in the kitchen doorway. Both fell into abashed silence. She looked from one to another. Both colored and dropped their eyes.

"I thought maybe I needed an extra cube of sugar," she remarked, "and no one seemed to be able to hear the kettle."

She crossed the room and switched off the gas.

Nick and Brent glowered at one another.

When the kettle settled to a low hollow sound, Mrs. Sawyer

turned. She said firmly, "Nick is going to do some work for me this summer."

"I heard," Brent said.

"Brent tells me he's going to be around all summer, too," Nick said. His voice was supercilious and mocking. It was obvious that he had not believed a word of the threat, and thought it was just one more instance of Brent's talking out his ass. He was eager to expose him.

Brent burned bright red; the absurdity of his hasty words repeated to him in front of his mother was humiliating.

Mrs. Sawyer, however, released the kettle and enveloped him in an enormous hug. She was almost dancing herself.

"Oh, honey, that's wonderful!" she crowed. She pushed him away to look at him and clapped her hands together. "What a *wonderful* idea!"

CHAPTER 7

Nick did not need the work. He had already been booked solid until November. It had been craziness to take this project on. Temporary insanity. He shot a rueful look back at the tired white house in his rearview mirror.

What was it that made him do such foolish things? He had told himself he was only joining Mrs. Sawyer for a cup of tea out of politeness. And he had been genuinely concerned that Brent was ill—even if part of him had felt that Brent deserved what he got.

Nick did not dislike Brent. Not personally. He was not necessarily a bad person. Just a weak one.

Nick repeated the words to himself as if he were trying them on for size. The pickup truck rumbled around a steady corner and out into a flat open field that was as familiar to Nick as his own hand.

Yes, that was it. Brent was a weak person. And that's what bothered Nick so much. That was what got under his skin.

But the thought of Brent draped in that quilt that barely covered him, the willful naughty exposure—it kept coming back to him as he drove. It made Nick want to spank him, to envelop him in his own body. Wrestle him. Dominate him. Teach him what was what. He wondered how someone as sensible as Mrs. Sawyer had ended up with such a son.

Over the next few days, Nick placed the order for the stone Mrs. Sawyer had wanted, and drew up a set of plans for her approval. They met again at the house.

Nick was wary. He had visions of Brent waking, stretching naked in the morning window, bare in the shower, the water cascading as he stretched and kneaded the muscles of his bare body. He imagined Brent looking out the upstairs window, meeting Nick's eyes, and caressing himself, stroking himself. His hot firm member poking out insolently from that small, equally firm body.

Nick found himself disappointed when Brent did not put in another appearance. The meeting was uneventful, and Mrs. Sawyer did not mention her son.

She reviewed the plans and asked thoughtful questions. She was looking to have a stone wall built around the small garden she kept to the side of the house near the shed. The project was simple enough and small in scope. But the ground was uneven and sloped, and Mrs. Sawyer insisted on a gated archway that could be latched against any animals that would otherwise steal the fruits of her garden.

Nick was no expert on agriculture, but he doubted his wall would prove effective against such pests. Deer, he pointed out, would easily leap it.

Mrs. Sawyer was adamant, insisting against all reason that it would give her peace of mind. "Humor an old woman," she finally advised. Nick gave in. He had done his duty and she had heard his counsel. He trusted that she was a wise enough woman—no doubt she had other reasons for building the wall around her tiny garden and it was not his place to ask.

Despite the pressure the project would put on his schedule, Nick was pleased to do the work for her. In fact, he explained to himself, as the starting date for the project approached and he had not again seen Brent, he had accepted exactly because Mrs. Sawyer was such a fine lady. She was the kind of mother he would have liked to have had. And an ideal client.

It had nothing to do with Brent. He had not even known Brent was going to be around. That was the truth. He was just doing his job.

The day he came to deliver the stone and stake out the borders of the gardens with wooden spikes and string, he did it first thing. Mrs. Sawyer had given him permission, assuring him she was up at five a.m. without fail.

Not Brent, Nick guessed. He's not the type likely to be an early riser. I bet he sleeps 'til noon.

He smiled in satisfaction at the sound of the stones cascading out of the delivery truck. They gave off sparks as they struck one another with tremendous force of gravity, and a little spiral of dust rose above them into the air.

This, Nick thought, would surely wake Brent from his bed. It would be good for him.

He glanced at the house, but the only person he had succeeded in rousing was Brent's twink little brother. He came out on the porch to look at the sound. He was determinedly unflappable, lounging, youthfully electric.

Nick frowned. Twinks were not his thing.

Adam shouted, "Brent's out in the way back, doing his yoga, if you're looking for him." He bit into the English muffin he was carrying. His face betrayed nothing.

Now why would he shout that, Nick wondered. Why should Nick be looking for Brent of all people? The little twink, he decided, was just trying to get a rise out of him.

But after Adam had jumped in the car of some trashy little high school girl, Nick left off from planting the stakes around the garden. He could not help from going out to the "way back," merely out of curiosity.

Brent had chosen a patch of sun on the sloped grass next to the frog pond. His shirt was on the lawn beside him. He was in bare feet and cargo shorts. His legs crossed in front of him, angled away from Nick toward the sun, rapt with concentration.

Was it possible, Nick thought, to be jealous of the sun?

Nick crouched by a beech tree, picking shelf fungus from the bark. He was quiet and still. Brent changed positions. Slowly. Inexorably. Glacier-like, unhurried changes. And impossible feats of stretching, which Nick admired as much for their athleticism as their eroticism. His eyes never left Brent's body.

Nick had to give credit where it was due. He did not grudge anyone his or her talents. It must have taken tremendous discipline to make one's body so obedient, a powerful mind to be so deep in rapture.

Maybe, he thought, there might be something redeemable in Brent, if only on Mrs. Sawyer's account. The seed rarely fell too far from the tree.

Nick's hands itched just to feel Brent's body. It was firm all over, from his face to his torso right down through the legs. His muscles were sculpted, perfectly crafted. They seemed to wink at him, shiny in the grass. Sparkle and glitter. He wanted so much to believe that the message it was sending was true.

And then an errant cloud passed over, and the faintest change of wind made Nick ashamed. He had been crouched here nearly twenty minutes. Wasting time. Not a lick of work done, as if he had all the time in the world.

He crept away, ashamed suddenly to be watching Brent instead of doing his own job. What on earth would he say if he were caught? What would he say to Mrs. Sawyer?

He knew in his heart of hearts that was a siren song. He could not believe it or give into it. He had to be strong. Stick with the plan. There would always be distractions. Those who finished the race were the ones who were strong enough to ignore them.

He was not afraid of sex with men. He had just never met one that was worthy.

Nick hurried through the rest of the staking as fast as he could, eager to finish before Brent did, as if Brent's supreme control and awareness would enable him to see what Nick had been doing. What he had been thinking. Not just here, but at night, when he stole away from Una's bed.

Strangely, though, as the day went on, the vision of Brent's firm body gave way to a grudging admiration for Brent's discipline. It inspired Nick to push himself even more than he was used to. He worked that day until he was worn tired, well after dusk, and he was amazed again at where a man might draw inspiration.

CHAPTER 8

A few days later, Brent put aside any regrets. He was actually beginning to look forward to the summer in Holmstead County, in a weird sort of way. It gave him a goal, a project for the summer—to drive Nick crazy.

Brent smiled at the idea. *Why not?* he thought. *Everybody has to have a hobby.*

Brent was in the Rite Aid in town, and had just plucked a bottle of bottled tan off the shelf, when he felt someone's eyes on him. Hard. Brent had a very developed awareness of when he was getting cruised.

Stalker? he thought. *Homicidal homophobe?*

Maybe it was Nick. Again. Since the day they had battled in his mother's kitchen, Brent had noticed Nick's lurking presence more than once. Near him. Almost, he imagined, inside him. As he sat in the way back yard by the frog pond and adopted a new yoga position—at that moment exactly, when his senses were at their most alert, their most fine-tuned, then he could feel Nick in the world with him. He did not think of him. He *sensed* Nick. A brooding presence—sultry, loping, like wolves at the edge of a light thrown by a campfire on an open wilderness. And there was a dark side of Brent that wanted to throw water on the fire and lay down on the smoldering logs and be torn apart.

Brent was still holding the bottle of self-tanner, still standing in place, and the eyes had not left him. It was not Nick. There was a less electric, less malevolent quality to this person, who he had not yet seen, but who was staring at him intensely across a rack of women's chalk-white hose.

Casually, giving away nothing, Brent put the tube he had been reading back on the shelf and then maneuvered himself so that he could look into the mirror above the rack of cheap $10 sunglasses.

"I thought so!" a voice boomed. It was a warm, wholehearted accusation. Brent was enveloped in a warm friendly hug and lifted off his feet so that both he and the hugger lost their balance and nearly toppled a rack of Hallmark cards over into the sunglasses.

"Bobby!" Brent exclaimed.

"Brent-buddy."

They stepped away from each other, looked each other up and down, and then collapsed again into a second hug. Bobby was a sight for sore eyes. He had always been able to turn Brent's whole mood upside down.

Bobby had hardly changed. He had the same round disheveled boyish look around his face, the same mop of dirty blond hair, the shorts (could it be the very same pair?) with skinned knees showing beneath from whatever latest goof he had gotten himself into. The worst damage turning thirty had inflicted on Bobby was a couple of crows feet around his eyes.

"Man, you look great!" Bobby said. "I hear you've been dancing all over. I've been meaning to take in a show, you know how it gets..."

"Thanks, Bobby. You don't look so bad yourself. It's nice to see someone besides me cares about how they look."

For a brief moment, an awkward silence dropped between them, as all their past caught up to them in a rush.

Then Brent spoke again, dispelling the awkward gloom of an unhappy past: "What are you doing here, man? Last I heard you had married Lisa and were living down in Sebago, or something. If I had known you were here, I'd have looked you up as soon as I got here. It's so good to see you!"

"You, too, man." He cocked his head, and smiled his lopsided smile. Then he dropped his voice. He drew Brent aside where he could speak more confidentially. "Yeah, well, me and Lisa, we're having our problems, you know what I mean?"

"Oh, sorry to hear that man."

"Yeah, we split. Just last month." Bobby looked like a dog that had been kicked. "Been almost a month now, and I was out of work anyhow, so I came home to the parents' place. Last night. Take a little time to sort things out, y'know?"

Brent nodded sympathetically.

"Your parents—they're well?"

"Yeah. Retirement is treating them right. They're away in Europe for a month, so I'm taking care of the house."

"They still live out by the lake in Winthrop?"

"Yup. Same old castle. Still have that concrete under the dock where we carved our initials."

Brent remembered acutely how he had wished so badly to draw a little heart around those initials and put a plus between them.

He said lamely, "Well, I'll have to come out there some time, drink some beers with you."

Bobby gave his dazzling trademark smile, clapping Brent on the back enthusiastically. "I'd like that, man, you should really do it."

They grinned at each other in mutually appreciative silence.

Then Brent faked a punch to the gut as he often saw straight guys do, laughed at himself, and asked, "So, what're you up to now, Bobby? Lemme buy you a coffee and let's dish."

"Dish?"

"Talk."

They sat in the coffee shop next door and talked about all the things they used to do when they were kids together in Holmstead County. Almost fifteen years since high school! Brent could hardly believe it. He felt a warmth for Bobby that had not diminished a bit.

And that was saying a lot. Back when they were kids, Brent had had a full-blown headlong crush on Bobby. Brent used to roll up against Bobby's body when they were camping. Or brush up against him when they were in bathing suits. He even remembered once climbing a tree behind Bobby and trying to look up his shorts.

And every time Bobby got one of the local girls to make out

with him, Brent pretended to be happy for Bobby, for getting to score. Even though each time tore out his heart. Brent wanted nothing more in the world than to be the girl Bobby married. To get kissed by Bobby, which he imagined would feel like heaven. One night out at the lake after they had stolen and drunk some of Bobby's parents' booze, Brent had blurted out that he loved him.

And then, as if he had to explain, added, "I mean, I'm *in love with you.*"

Brent had assumed the admission would drive Bobby away. He had looked at it as plunging a dagger into his heart. The end of all things.

But, of course, it had no such dramatic effect.

Bobby said, "Really?!" He seemed to find it interesting. It fed his vanity. "What do you like about me?"

That night, they had gone skinny-dipping. Bobby had peeled off his clothes by the side of the lake, under the moonlight. His pale skin glistened. His young body was beautiful and firm—the most beautiful thing, Brent had told him, that he had ever seen.

Bobby only smiled. The whole time he had been undressing, he had been looking at Brent, knowing it was killing Brent to watch and not to touch. He stood naked for Brent for what seemed like ages.

Then, suddenly, Bobby had jumped in the water. The splashing cold droplets struck Brent on the cheek like tears. Bobby swam off in a luminous phosphorescence caused by the moonlight.

Brent had hurled himself after Bobby like a man hurls himself from a cliff. He had shouted and hollered, as if by volume alone he could drown out his hurt feelings. His sadness and loneliness and desperation. *Will I ever be loved? Will Bobby ever love me?*

And Brent tried to pretend he was not humiliated. He had tried to pretend he was not heartbroken. Instead, Brent had spent his senior year in like a widow in mourning, wearing black lipstick that made Heidi shake her head and advise him that he was getting weirder and weirder.

What was strange, Brent was thinking to himself as he listened to Bobby talk in the coffee shop fifteen years later, was how he had ever let himself be driven to such a point of desperation by this guy. What had he been thinking?!

Sure, Bobby was cute and lanky in a boyish sort of way. He was as friendly and flirty as ever before. But there did not seem to be much spark in him of the kind that Brent usually fell for in his adult life—not much sense of true, quiet confidence that came to someone when they understood their place in life and their goals and were well on their way to getting them.

"I missed you, man," he heard Bobby say, and the words startled Brent into the present. Into wakefulness. "You were the best friend a guy could ever have had."

Brent smiled back, skeptical, as if what Bobby said was what Bobby thought he wanted to hear, that same old empty flirtatiousness.

With little prodding, Brent was able to steer the conversation back toward his split with his wife. Bobby was eager for the chance to talk.

"It looked hopeless," he complained. "Permanent." He shrugged. "It's hard to see how we could get back together he said. The spark is gone. I don't think we love each other anymore."

He shook his head from side to side, eyes lowered in defeat at this turn of events that life had dealt him. Then he looked up.

"Maybe I should have gone your way, man," he said, desperately. "I mean with boys. It would have saved me a whole lot of trouble. I get along with guys so much better."

Brent laughed. At him. It amazed him whenever straight people imagined being gay was somehow easier.

"No, really, man," Bobby insisted. He seemed put out that Brent did not take him seriously, and spoke with a low immediate urgency. "I mean, I look at you, you're successful, you're in better shape than you ever were." Bobby reached out and squeezed Brent's arm. "Man, you're like a rock."

Brent was at a loss for words.

Bobby continued to talk with that same burning persuasive

urgency. "I mean, I've been thinking about it a lot, man. You and I always got along so well. I mean, we were best friends for years! And you had such a big heart..."

Brent tried to force himself to listen to Bobby's speeches with the skepticism they deserved. Still, something deep inside Brent made him yearn to make Bobby happy. Not to believe him and his flattery, necessarily. But to give him comfort. To touch and soothe him.

Brent was convinced he would always feel that yearning. He would always have a special place in his heart for Bobby. It was part of what made a first crush so puppyish, that warm tide of resurgent feeling you could not help and never quite got over, no matter how long you lived.

No matter how long you tried to tell yourself that broken hearts were supposed to heal.

After Bobby left, Brent sat in the coffee shop and finished his coffee and watched the half-familiar faces come in and out. Brent was almost disappointed at having run into Bobby. He would never again be able to pretend that Bobby was his true love. Bobby could become a full-time, flag-waving, card-carrying, ass-fucking homosexual and still never be Brent's husband. Brent was different than he had been. More mature. His tastes had changed.

Brent carried that warm, sad flood of feeling through the door of the coffee house out into the direct June sunshine, where he stood blinking, stunned by the brightness of the summer afternoon and the noisy mayhem out on the sidewalk. He had walked unwittingly into a melee of dropped ice cream cones and teeming children.

Nick, of all people, was standing in the middle of a cluster of children. He had one kid on his shoulders wanting to get down, another kid on the sidewalk trying to clamber up his trouser leg, a third yanking on his free hand, and an upturned ice cream cone on the sidewalk rapidly melting.

Nick was beleaguered, harried, his hair a mess, his eyes desperate. He was trying to keep up with each of the kids and do all things at once. That tremendous glacial calm so fitting in a man who worked with granite had been surrendered entirely to the frantic necessity of trying to please and discipline three competing children at once.

"We are NOT going back," he was saying. "You need to be more careful, you always drop your cone, Deidre, every single time."

The speech produced a whine of almost cosmically anguished proportions from the child on his shoulders, who in frustration gripped hard on Nick's hair—a grip, Brent thought automatically, that he would not mind having, albeit in a more sexual situation.

Nick looked up wildly, left, right, hardly seeming to see what was in front of him.

Brent covered the laugh that was escaping his mouth.

"Welcome," he called out, "to the joys of fatherhood. Sure you don't want to change your mind? There's always time to go back."

Nick was relieved to have a place to direct his anger, and he began, "Last thing I need...." Then—after re-evaluating his precarious situation—he seemed to think better of delivering that particular speech.

"Could you take one of these kids, please?" he begged.

Brent remained doggedly still.

"I'm not the one trying to become a straight man, remember?"

"Please."

Nick fixed him with a look that was so heart-rendingly pathetic and pleading that Brent could not resist.

"OK, OK, I give up." Brent approached and looked each of the kids in the face. He adopted a curious exaggerated expression and stroked his non-existent beard in an imitation of deep thought and studied consideration.

Even the child on Nick's shoulders fell silent at this curious lithe stranger, who was examining them with such exaggerated and scientific care. Their mouths fell open and silent mid-scream.

"So, which one of you guys is the very best one?" Brent asked in a twisted accent, half-Germanic, half- mad scientist. "I only vant to take zee very best." He zeroed in on the one on Nick's shoulders. "Is it...you?"

The girl giggled.

Brent whirled and directed his index finger at the one standing, holding Nick's hands, who appeared both to be the most naturally shy, and the bravest at the same time.

"Or is it...you?"

The little girl shrank, but announced defiantly, "We're all good!"

"You're all good?!!" Brent made a face, like he was going to explode, said "Overload, overload!" in a funny computerized voice, and then did a standing flip on the spot.

The children's eyes bulged. The one on Nick's shoulder giggled. Brent knelt so he was at the child's level.

"Then I'm going to have to take each and every one of you, I guess!"

He gently disengaged the two on the ground from Nick's hands. The one on Nick's shoulders said, "I wanna go, too!"

Dutifully, Nick let that one to get ground as if she weighed nothing at all, and she jumped and harried Brent's legs.

"Well," Brent said, "this is going to have to be the biggest hug in the world to get you all in it!" And he put his arms around them all and squeezed out a raft of giggles. The children began to poke and mess up his hair, and Brent pretended to gnash his teeth and laugh and cry and make strange faces.

Nick was in genuine awe of Brent's transformation of the children from ranting crybabies to giggling putty in his hands.

Brent met his eye. "Why don't you make yourself useful, 'Dad,' and buy the child another ice cream cone?"

Nick did not hesitate to obey.

That's what I like, Brent thought, *a man who can take orders.*

By the time Nick returned with the ice cream, Brent had learned his young charges names: Deidre, Fiona, and Colm.

"You must be a set of leprechauns, then!" he accused.

The younger children giggled and the older one was disapproving. "We're Irish!" she said crossly.

"Amish? Impish? Emp Fish?"

The children howled in protest.

Brent said stubbornly, "No, I think you're really Leprechauns. I really do. And I can prove it!"

The children giggled again and did not deny it, and Brent held one of them upside down and shook her hoping coins from her pot of gold would spill out.

"Where's your pot of gold, missy?"

"Hey, hey, hey, careful, there, you don't want her to get hurt," Nick called, hurrying down the road from the ice cream parlor.

"Don't be a party-pooper, 'Dad'," Brent said. And the kids launched into a rambunctious chorus of "party-pooper, party-pooper" over and over.

Nick sighed, defeated. He bent at the waist and handed over the cone, which Fiona accepted shyly.

Brent poked her. "What do you say, your highness?"

"Thank you."

"You're welcome," Nick said. His voice was deep and round, the sound of a kettledrum, and quite soothing. At least Brent was soothed. The children seemed interested in more antic, leprechaun games.

"May I?" Brent asked, nodding his head toward the park across the street,

"Their mother..." Nick started to say, and then relented. "Sure, go ahead. You've got ten."

"Uh-oh," Brent said, "Speed leprechaun games!" And he led the gaggle of little Irish children into a screaming frolic in the park, dancing and dodging and poking, until they were all collapsed and out of breath. He fell to the ground and let the kids pin him down.

Nick stood by the rail around the park, leaning over, watching the games. A thoughtful look rested on his face.

"You waiting for an invite? Come on in," Brent shouted.

Nick hesitated, glanced behind him as if Big Brother was watching.

"We don't bite?" He looked at the kids, crossed his eyes and growled. "Much." And made a big show of snapping his jaws at them, which produced another gale of tired laughter.

Nick vaulted the fence, ambled over to a spot nearby and flopped down on the grass. Again, Brent marveled at the way he moved. Despite his size, he had the fluid, long-limbed grace of a ballerina or a palm frond.

Brent dispatched the children to go hunt for more gold in the swings. Then he took up a seat next to Nick, cross-legged, at what he judged to be an unkissable distance.

"You have quite a way with kids," Nick said.

"Yes, well, I've had some experience, you know."

Nick looked positively alarmed. "You have?!"

"Not my own, fool. My little brother, Adam. He's ten years younger than me. You know the drill. The 'Mistake' my parents never meant to have. And my mother was sick when he was growing up, so I basically raised him myself."

"That must have been hard." There was a note of genuine sympathy, even loneliness in Nick's voice.

Brent shrugged. "Not really. I didn't think twice about it. And I had a bunch of sisters around as back-up. And there was only one of him. Besides, it gives me something to tease the kid about when he gets high and mighty."

"Well...I think that's great. You really...have a way with them. You almost look like one of them, when you're all playing there together."

"Um...thanks."

"No, I mean...not because you're short...because you get all excited like them, you have all this energy. And you're not very big, too..."

Brent flexed his bicep. "Watch it, Mister. I'm bigger than I look. I would hate to have to beat you up."

Nick smiled in his slow, controlled way. Brent swore he could actually see the thoughtful reassessment taking place behind his eyes.

"So, do you like children, Nick?"

Nick colored. "I don't know anything about them," he admitted. "I don't know any. And I didn't even have any brothers and sisters. I was an only child."

An uneasy peace fell between them, and this time Brent did not break it with random conversation, for fear he would only succeed in annoying or embarrassing Nick. Nick plucked a blade of grass and chewed it like a farm boy, wheat-end out. Brent pictured him in a pair of overalls, with one strap undone and nothing on beneath.

"Did you ever think of having kids of your own?" Nick asked.

Brent stirred from his private fantasies. He said carefully, "That's a decision for the future. I'm putting all my energies into finding my husband first. One step at a time, right?"

They were lying side by side, both watching the children and not each other. Brent started doing a few stretches. Limber as always, he could fold himself nearly in two.

"So, you don't have a man, now?"

Brent shot him a glance from underneath his stretched arm. "I'd hardly have been flirting with you, Nick, if I had a man now."

"Is that what we're doing?" Nick asked sharply.

"Relax, cowboy. I meant before I discovered you were an uptight, closeted asshole, remember? Now, we're just babysitting together."

A wry look twisted Nick's lips and he nodded, although what portion of Brent's comment he was agreeing with, Brent could not be sure.

"I didn't think that having a man at home usually kept gay guys from flirting," he said. "Or worse."

"Sounds like a tale from the annals of bad personal experience."

Nick fixed him with a quick, almost frightened look. "Don't

read too much into it. I'm just saying. Lot of gay guys aren't exactly what you call models of loyalty, and I thought...."

"You thought I was one of them," Brent finished smoothly for him.

"Well, the way you..."

"No, don't apologize. You thought what you thought. I don't deny that when I'm single, I like to flirt. Why not? It's fun. I might even go beyond flirting."

Brent let the suggestion hang in the air between them like a ripe fruit that begged to be plucked. It was clear from Nick's face that he did not miss the implication.

Brent added, "But I don't cheat. Ever. That's where I draw the line. Where other people draw it is their business...unless they're dating me, then it's my business, too."

"I think cheaters are the worst kind of people."

"I bet you think a lot of things." He could not resist adding, "I don't go around judging people indiscriminately. I'm sure they have their reasons." He almost kicked himself as the words came out; the superior tone and content belonged entirely to Heidi.

"There's never a reason for cheating," Nick said stubbornly. Then his face cracked in a smile. "Besides, of course you go around judging people indiscriminately. You judged me without knowing a thing about me. You judge every single person in this County when you write it off as less than your superior little city life."

"Well, maybe once or twice," Brent allowed, "I've been known to judge."

"But only when they deserve it?"

"Exactly."

Brent let his eyes close, and the lazy heat of the afternoon gathered around him. He heard the tone of an ice cream truck, and the creak of swings on rusted hinges.

"What about that guy you were with in the coffee shop?" Nick persisted. "Was he one of your prospective husbands?"

Brent rolled his head so he could look Nick in the face,

"You spying on me, Nick?"

"Don't be ridiculous. I happened to see you when we passed on the way to the ice cream shop. You're hard to miss."

"Thank you."

"I meant, you're hard to miss because you've got the city written all over you."

"Now who's judging by surfaces?"

"So is he?"

"Not anymore."

"You dated him?"

"I wouldn't call it dating."

Nick's lips tightened in disapproval.

"Oh, don't get so high and mighty...I was seventeen years old. I thought I was in love."

"So he's gay?"

"I wished he was."

"What does that mean?"

Brent again closed his eyes. "He's a straight man who wants attention."

"That's redundant."

Brent opened his eyes again, bright with amusement. "Careful, we just might make a certified citified bitch-queen out of you yet, Nick."

This assessment did not seem to upset Nick. In fact, he seemed quite pleased with the compliment.

"Why are you suddenly so filled with smiles, Mr. Happy."

"Me? I'm not happy." Nick drew a mask over his face, looking as guilty suddenly as if Brent had caught him masturbating.

If I didn't know better, Brent thought, *I would have guessed he was happy because me and Bobby are not together.*

Lying back in the grass, Brent let his arms fling wide. At that very moment, Nick had reached out to pluck a new blade of grass. Their hands made contact, and Nick drew back as if he had touched a live electric wire.

Nick made a show out of checking his watch. He held his

other hand, the one Brent had touched, close to his side as if it were wounded.

"Well," he said, "got to go." He jumped up. "Thank you so much for doing that. For taking care of the kids."

Brent, too, rustled himself to his feet. Nick stuck out a hand. Boyishly. Frat-ishly, Brent thought, but he took the hand anyway.

"Really," Nick said. "I mean it. That was very...nice of you."

"Well, you know what they say about nice guys...."

"No, what?" Nick called out for each of the children in a slow almost lyrical bellow. His voice rang out like peels of thunder, and it made Brent's belly twitch.

"What do they say about nice guys? They say nice guys suck a mean cock," he said rapidly, and then he scurried quickly away before the outrage had settled on Nick's face.

CHAPTER 9

Heidi Sawyer understood Nick's silence. She understood that there were things that were not proper to talk about, but she never pretended they did not exist. He showed up at Heidi's dinner table more and more often on the way home from Mrs. Sawyer's place. Each time, he updated her on what he was doing at Mrs. Sawyer's, until she stifled a yawn and he realized he had stayed too late. He apologized for running on at the mouth, and she assured him no, he should come again. She said how glad she was that Nick was doing the job and not someone else who did not have his appreciation for quality.

Una complained about Nick's regular dinners with Heidi, until she heard that Brent had not been there. Una said, "Heidi is on our side."

She turned her face to him for a kiss. He closed his arms around her, nearly lifting her from her feet, and brought her close so she could no longer see his face.

Nick thought: *Even if I wanted Brent—AND I DON'T—but even if I wanted him, I could not have him. That was not part of the plan.*

He squeezed Una gently, and wished he could squeeze harder. He brushed her backside affectionately. He wished for a moment that he had some ardor to give her. Some passion.

But that was not what their life was based on. It was based on planning and mutual need. A house they would set up to raise children, and maybe some day grandchildren. A safe place for both of them. Una would get her citizenship and have a career. Nick would grow the business to a comfortable size.

This was what Nick wanted. To provide for someone. To put a roof over their head and food on the table. To watch kids grow and prosper. He had wanted it all his life. It was all a big happily-ever-after. Win-win. And Nick knew he could not get that anywhere else in the world, except from Una.

The next morning Nick was back at work at Mrs. Sawyer's. His eyes swept the face of the house as if he might catch a glimpse of Brent hidden behind the windows.

Brent's little brother appeared on the door step and said, "He's not here. He's out with an old buddy of his. They're out on the lake."

These unexpected words struck home.

The last stone Nick had placed on the wall came rolling down. He had to jump to avoid getting his toes crushed.

Adam laughed.

Nick growled, "Go on, stop bothering me, you twerp, or I'll give you something to laugh about." He bent to retrieve the errant stone.

Who was this old buddy? What were they doing? Did Nick know him? Was he attractive? Nick had been wrestling with the strange, jarring, unsettling feeling that he had got watching Brent at play with Una's children. It was as if Nick were seeing another world, another time, an alternate universe.

He had to fight through this and focus on what was good and true.   Nick hefted the rock from the ground and again placed it carefully on the wall. He moved it just fractions of an inch this way and that until he found the place where it fit most firmly. Then he stepped back to survey where he would place the next stone in succession, working three moves ahead like a chess player, until he had exhausted the pile of loose rock, or had finished the project.

Considering the stone he had just placed, Nick thought with pride: *I have been through life. With Una I have found the place where I fit most firmly.*

He thought: *Brent would get bored with my kind of life.*

He lifted another stone and placed it next to the first. He felt a small vibration in it, a wobble so faint most people would not have noticed it. But to Nick, it meant that there was a weakness hidden in the wall.

He could easily have ignored the problem. No one besides him would know. It would be twenty years before the stones spilled prematurely to the ground because of the imbalance.

But Nick disassembled what he had been working on. It took three hours before he was satisfied that he had undone the problem. Nick built things to last. He built for himself, every time.

Using fury and sexual energy, he continued to work all afternoon, until he discovered he had somehow walled himself in.

CHAPTER 10

In the early 19th century, Holmstead County had been an industrial center. The many steep rivers provided an abundant source of power for the factories. Along their banks were the wrecks and foundations of early mills, some with waterwheels intact.

The first and most famous of these industries was watchmaking. It was in New England that clocks and watches were first mass-produced, and made cheap enough for every household in America to have one. Holmstead County was Watch City until the last factory closed in the nineteen fifties. Even now, the County celebrated its heritage with the annual Parade of Clocks. It was a carnival, attracting a weird agglomeration of e-hippies and stick-in-the-mud conservatives.

It had been years since Brent had come to the Parade of Clocks. He was torn between dressing as an old grandfather clock and a clock with a face as large as a monster sunflower. He made a pest of himself surveying his sisters, his sisters' children, his mother, Bobby, and just about anyone he met.

Ultimately, with the kids' help, he constructed a massive dial, almost four feet in radius, with giant numbers, and an hour hand longer than his own arms. The whole thing slid over his head, so that his eyes were two holes in the center of the dial.

The kids clapped wildly when he put it on, and Brent made the giant hands spin in appreciative delight. At the carnival, Brent had a great old time snarling traffic, and his sisters' children were all in tow, looking—given their relatively diminutive size and matching clock-face costumes—like little dandelions.

Brent called them his Little Weeds. They all had a great time, until Brent got into a confrontation with a Cadillac bearing New York plates. Brent stepped in front of the car, his back to its front bumper, so that his Little Weeds could safely get across the street.

The driver yelled something rude out the window.

Brent snapped back.

"What did you say?" snarled the driver.

Brent turned slowly and majestically. Given the size of his costume, it was like trying to change the direction of an ocean liner and took a few moments to get around.

"I said, go fuck yourself, ya fat dickweed. If you wanta hurry, go back to New York. Here time stands still." One of the Little Weeds darted back across the street. "Sometimes it even goes backward," Brent joked. He yelled after the guilty little weed to come back.

The driver was not amused. He leaped from his car, strode up to Brent and began to yell at him, poking him in the chest with his finger.

Brent yelled back, letting loose his best stream of Chelsea-bar bitchery. Pretty soon, a crowd had gathered around. Brent and the driver were head to head, arguing vociferously, even as Brent tried to keep an eye out for his Little Weeds.

Because of the giant orange clock-face costume, however, Brent could not see where he was going. He stumbled into a pothole. His knee buckled and he went down hard, clutching at the knee, and bracing for the white-hot flash of pain.

The crowd collectively gasped. The New Yorker was taken aback. He fell into silence. The Weeds cried out, and one of them ran up to the New Yorker and began to kick his shin.

Holding off the angry Little Weed, the New Yorker again directed a renewed tirade at Brent.

At that moment, a shadow thrown from a sequoia fell over Brent where he lay. Instantly, the New Yorker went silent.

"Is there a problem here?" Nick asked. His voice was like thunder. He stood with his legs planted far apart, his arms hanging loosely by his side, his fingers half-curled as if they itched to make a fist.

The New Yorker explained that he had just been trying to get through.

"So am I," Nick said.

The New Yorker looked pleased, as if he had discovered an ally. He spoke about what a pain in the ass the whole Parade was, and why they could not keep it to side streets, and on and on, rattling at the mouth for his increasingly disgusted audience.

Nick reached down and lifted Brent to his feet. Turning to the New Yorker, he growled menacingly, "But I don't go knocking people to the ground to do it."

"I didn't knock him to the ground..." the New Yorker whined.

Brent also protested this characterization, embarrassed that Nick would think this gut-fat New Yorker had gotten the better of him.

Before Nick could act, Una elbowed through the crowd. She looked at Brent, then at the New Yorker, and then at Nick. She tugged his arm. She had warned him not to leave the car, not to get involved. She flailed at him, insisting that they go about their business. There were the children to think about.

Nick silenced her with a look. He ordered the New Yorker back to his car. Nick told Brent and the Little Weeds to get out of the road and stay there. The others in the crowd also reluctantly made way, and the New Yorker drove through the Red Sea that Nick had parted.

Good humor was restored and a pair of clocks began to dance in the street. Brent attempted to readjust his giant clock face costume. It had been irreparably damaged in the fall. The hands were bent and pointing out, and one side had been partially sheared off.

While he fussed with the costume, he noticed that Una had got hold of Nick and was bodily forcing him back to their car. He jumped, told the Little Weeds not to move, and shuffled at full speed toward their car.

He wanted to assure Nick that he had not needed any help. That he had not been pushed to the ground. That he had just fallen, no damage to the knee. He had been just about to KO that New York son-of-a-bitch.

As Nick's car pulled from the curb, Brent tore off his costume and threw himself in front of the car. In the backseat, Una's kids clapped with joy.

Nick rolled down the driver's side window.

"Yes?"

"I just wanted to, well, thank you for stepping in. Not because I was afraid something was going to happen. If you had just held him off for ten minutes so I could get free of this costume. I would have been ready to fight."

"No fight was necessary."

"Well...aren't you quite the diplomat!"

"When you're my size," Nick explained, "people like to pick fights. So you either get good at fighting or you get good at negotiating."

Una leaned across Nick's lap. "Nick's done a bit o' both," she said. She made it clear that she possessed him, staring Brent in the face, triumphant, as if she had taken home the big prize.

Brent introduced himself. "Heard a lot about you," he said.

Her hand was like a fish, but Brent was determined to win her over. He mentioned the beautiful children, but she snapped that she did not approve of allowing them to play on dangerous swings at the park.

"Nice to have met you," Brent said. This made Nick laugh, genuinely. Brent flushed. The laugh was an unexpected pleasure.

He didn't want the conversation to end. As Nick inched away through the heavy traffic, Brent walked alongside the car, babbling about how Nick should have joined the parade, since he would have made the best grandfather clock ever.

"I've got no time for these games," Nick said. "Got a project to finish before the wedding. Not a big fan of this foolishness."

"Maybe you need a little foolishness," Brent proposed.

"My best customers are the kind you just drove off," Nick replied.

"Oh, lighten up. It's just like another Halloween. Didn't you like Halloween, Nick? Or did the other kids steal all your candy?"

"I don't do costumes. I have no desire to be something other than what I am."

Una was a bruised and purple color.

"Nick!" she said.

"I—We've got to go, Brent."

Brent stepped back. Nick rolled up the window and put the car in gear.

Reluctantly, Brent thought. *He pulled away reluctantly. I swear it.*

When Brent turned, his sisters were on the curb behind him, surrounded by their various offspring. They were staring malevolently.

"Shall I get you witches, um, I mean ladies, a cauldron you can all stand around?"

They began to berate Brent for leaving the children and for harassing Nick and for every little sin of his childhood.

"That's it, girls, stir the cauldron! Stir it up!"

After his sister had taken the Little Weeds off to pack them up for the night, Brent felt lonely. He held up the costume in front of him. It flopped lifelessly.

Distinctly warped and weathered, he thought. *Like I'm going to be sooner or later.*

Tick-tock. Time was passing. Years of life wasted. And no prospect of a husband. No chance of Mr. Right.

"I'm going to end up gay, bitter, and all alone," he said to the face of his costume, and then proceeded to draw it over his head, like a paper bag.

"Hey!"

Brent struggled through the sleeves of his costume and peered out through the neck hole toward the voice that had spoken. Bobby was standing there, swaying drunkenly. He had not bothered to put on a costume, but it was obvious that that fact had not kept him from celebrating.

"You look a little droopy," he said.

"Amen."

"Why don't we go have some drinks?"

"It's getting late. I need to get back to my mother's and...."

"What? You going to turn into a pumpkin?" Bobby adjusted the bent arms of Brent's costume clock backward a few hours. "Now," he said, "you've got all the time in the world."

Brent smiled. It was like the old days, Bobby leading him astray.

"My mother's gonna hate you," Brent said.

"She already hates me," Bobby said cheerfully. "Let's go get a drink."

They picked up plastic Parade-of-Clocks "to-go" cups from Dairy Queen and filled them at the Irish bar at the end of the block. Then they walked around the dwindling crowd, alternately making fun of and making friends with strangers.

Bobby's cheerful inanity was infectious. Brent's depression quickly dissipated. They refilled their cups as they went, and Bobby never seemed to get any drunker, no matter how many times he filled up.

"I see you've still got the cast iron stomach."

"Practice makes perfect. You?"

"I may weigh a hundred forty pounds wet," Brent vowed, "but the gay gene includes an ability to drink as well as suck cock. Goes with the territory."

They swung from street signs and lampposts, and kicked at cans in the street, like two Holmstead County country boys with no worries in the world.

It would never be like this with Nick, Brent thought. *Nick and I are too different.*

The stalls that had been set up for selling antiques and crafts—quilts, lamps, and, of course, clocks—began to fold up for the night and pack away their wears.

"Isn't it amazing?" Brent said, pointing to the many clocks

for sale. "Not a single one of these clocks is produced in the United States any more. Not one."

"So what?"

"So what? It's like time was stolen from us," Brent comments. "Holmstead County used to be a hotbed of clock-making. And now what? Nothing! No jobs!"

"You don't have to tell me, I've been looking for one for weeks."

"We should take it all back," Brent proposed. Rebellion and mischief were in his voice, and the vendor, an old man in a nylon windbreaker eyed them warily.

"Don't you boys be getting any ideas," the vendor growled.

"Let me set the clocks back to the times of yore!" Brent begged, realizing for the first time that he was very drunk.

"Time is a one-way street, gentlemen. And it only runs faster as you get older, which you young ones will learn soon enough." He unlatched the plywood door that covered the opening of his vending booth and pulled it down over everything inside. "If it's time you want to capture, capture the time you're in. It ain't coming back."

This seemed so wise to Brent and Bobby that they begged the old man to join them for a drink. He only smiled wisely, snapped the padlock home, and wished them a good night.

"You know," Brent predicted, "if we come back here next year, I bet we'll never find his cart again. He never really existed. Just a wise apparition, like hearing the wisdom of God."

Bobby threw his arm around Brent's shoulders. Only little pockets of people were left on the sidewalks from the crowds earlier in the day. Their bodies bumped and swayed against one another, and Brent felt as if his legs were holding up the both of them.

They stumbled upon the gazebo in the town square. Bobby kicked back and stretched out, feet splayed out as if he was in his own living room. Bobby looked pleased with what they had done, another day well spent. He poked Brent in the gut.

"It's so good to talk to you, man," he said. "We get along so easily. I mean, I haven't seen you in like ten years and it's like no time passed."

"True friends," Brent murmured.

"It's not like that with my wife, man. Talking to her is such a chore," he sighed. "We really were not meant for one another."

Bobby looked yearningly at Brent.

Brent flushed. He was flattered but uncomfortable. *This was booze talking,* he thought. *Nothing worse than when the booze gets all affectionate.*

Bobby slid closer, so that his hip was pressed up against Brent's side. He took Brent's hand in his. Bobby was gazing into his face from two inches away.

Then, inevitably, Bobby kissed him full on the lips. With boyish confidence, he licked his own lips and said, "I could get used to that."

Bobby's still a little teenager, a little flirt, Brent thought. *A boy who never failed to be excited that he made it to first base.*

The kiss did nothing for him.

Each relationship has one chance, Brent thought, *one moment to kindle into a greater fire.*

If you miss the moment, nothing will happen, no matter how hard you try. That wise man was right. Time was all one way.

Bobby said, "I love you, man." And then he was gone into the night.

Brent rested quietly, wondering how it would feel to sleep in the gazebo all night, when Heidi's voice roused him from reverie.

"Good God!" she said. "There you are! I've been looking all over. We're going to head out. Do you want a ride back to Mom's?"

She climbed up into the bandstand.

"How'd you know it was me?"

"Brent, I could see you in the pitch dark and know it was you. No one moves like you. You've got that signature...Hey!"

Brent smiled.

"You're drunk!"

"A little. How can you tell?"

"One look at your face is all it takes." She plopped down beside him. She took one more look, and then made the correct diagnosis: "You're in love."

"Don't be so ridiculous," Brent said, struggling again to shed his costume. "Who am I going to fall in love with up here?"

She was silent and did not answer. And then said ruminatively, "Why do gay men always pursue the unattainable?"

"Oh, bullshit," Brent shot back, irritable and pouty, like a child whose secret had been stolen, or who was required to share his toys with the other kids.

"It's true," she insisted.

"Nonsense. What you straight people see as unattainable, we call high standards. We aren't willing to settle for just anybody with a pulse."

Heidi's face fell, and Brent felt instantly guilty. "Oh, for God's sake, woman! I'm not talking about Gar! Don't take it so personally. I love Gar. Gar rocks."

For a moment she was quiet. The night, too, was quiet, punctuated only by the odd yell or the roar of a motor coming to life.

Heidi began to sob.

"It's the biggest mistake of my life!" she cried out.

"You're drunk, too."

She nodded.

"Typical case of post-marital depression," he diagnosed.

"I know," she said, "I know. We're all crazy."

"Who?"

"Our family. Everybody. Whoever."

"Everybody," Brent agreed fervently. "I kissed Bobby."

"You kissed Bobby?!"

He nodded.

"We *all* wanted to kiss Bobby when we were little girls!" She laughed. "Get out! Don't tell me..."

"Oh, of course not."

"Good. I was worried..."

"Worried that it was him I was in love with?"
"Yes."
"I'm over it, trust me."
"You have too big a heart to be over anyone."

CHAPTER 11

The warning beeps from a truck backing up the driveway penetrated Brent's sleep. Then, suddenly, there was a great roar of tumbling rock. Brent sat bolt upright in bed.

Out in the driveway, a dumptruck was poised in the morning sun, its bed tipped back, and a mountain of huge stones on the ground beneath. The driver was standing there, boot on the back bumper. He was jawing away with Nick, a cup of coffee in his hand.

Brent ran down and burst through the front door. He stood in front of them like a vampire, squinting viciously in the sunlight.

"Good morning!" Nick boomed. He was looking at Brent with frank appreciation.

Brent looked down at himself. He was wearing nothing but the pair of tighty-whities he had been sleeping in.

"It's not morning yet. What time is it? Three? Four a.m.?"

"Seven. Did I wake you?"

Brent wished Nick would turn the volume down a notch on his booming voice. The syllables were crashing into one another and reverberating around his head like a percussion band.

"I think I went to bed about an hour ago." It was true. He and Heidi and Gar had stayed up most of the night dancing in their living room. "What are you doing here?"

"I work here. Remember? Today's the day I promised your mother I would, and I'm always good to my word." He turned and waved his arm at the load of stone. "This is the last of it!"

"Thank the good Lord. But couldn't you have waited until noon?"

Mrs. Sawyer appeared at the back door with a cup of coffee for Nick.

"Brent Sawyer! For heaven's sake! Put some clothes on!"

Brent retreated upstairs with his hands placed over his ears to drown out the bitchery. He felt their eyes on his backside, one lusty, the other pair disapproving.

"They both," he thought boldly, "can kiss my ass."

"A touch of the Irish flu, that's what he's got" Nick said. "That's what Una always says."

Mrs. Sawyer laughed delightedly.

Brent popped a couple of aspirin, drank three gallons of cold water, and pulled the pillow over his head as if he was going to stifle himself. When he woke again four hours later, Brent felt improved. It was a much more civilized hour. *If I was back in the city,* he thought, *I would just now be going for a pajama brunch. And perhaps order a Mimosa to take the edge off.*

Mrs. Sawyer was out in the garden fighting off a Biblical plague of Japanese beetles that were threatening her roses. Nick was in the back yard, stripped to the waist beneath the hot sun. His skin was bronzed and glistening, the fine hair of his forearms gold as grain. His hair was wet with sweat.

Brent pulled back his mother's lace curtains for a better view. His cock swelled in his trousers. This was a brunch for which he had a healthy appetite.

Brent had settled in for a leisurely viewing, but the movement of lace must somehow have caught Nick's eye. Nick whirled. Brent was caught red-handed. And red-faced.

"Hey," Brent said weakly through the open window.

"Good morning again," said Nick. "You peeping?"

"Just...uh...adjusting the curtains."

"Oh. I did see that they were a mess. Feeling better?"

"Excellent. Outstanding. Tip-top. A-number one."

"I think I'd enjoy the conversation better," Nick suggested, "if I was looking at a face rather than talking to a window frame."

Brent let the curtain fall. He came out into the backyard, but not without first stopping by the kitchen for coffee to show that he was not in too much of a hurry. You can't, he had learned in a decade of dating gay men, let them think you're too eager.

By the time he got back outside, Nick had gone back to work. *He doesn't waste a moment of his time,* Brent thought. *I'll bet he always gets off first.*

"I'm disappointed," Nick said.

"Me, too," Brent said. "What are you disappointed about?"

"I liked your earlier sartorial choices much better."

"'Sartorial?'" Brent scoffed. "Who says 'sartorial' when you mean a pair of bikini briefs?"

"I thought it lent you a certain dignity not otherwise apparent."

"Dignity is overrated. I stand proud in my tighty-whities."

"Certain parts of you prouder than others."

Brent blushed at the thought of his morning wood. "That's good," he said appreciatively. "It takes a lot to make me blush."

He pulled aside a loose stone and sat down on it. Nick continued to work. He conversed steadily, but all the while his eyes were moving over the pile of stone the dumptruck had left behind. Prodding. Judging. Turning shapes over in his head.

"What's the rush?" Brent asked.

"I promised your mother I'd have it done today. I never promise anything I cannot deliver."

Brent had not realized how close Nick was to being finished. The clock was ticking. Brent suggested, "You may have underestimated the time my mother requires in quality gossip-time."

"No, that I factored in. It was her son's needs in that regard that I failed to appreciate."

He stared pointedly at where Brent was sitting on his ass. Brent grinned. He liked a guy that gave as good as he got. "*Somebody's* been busy practicing his bitchery...."

Nick smiled.

"So we've rented a sense of humor for the morning," Brent said. "How nice. How long can we expect it to stay?"

Nick did not immediately answer, and Brent sipped his coffee and watched Nick work in silence. He was magnificent. Melon pecs. Downward pointed nipples, small and round. Meaty swaths of lean muscle up his side. A basket of hard abs stretched across his ribs. The smell of his sweat in the air.

Imagine what he's like in the sack!

"Is this it? Just rocks?" Brent asked politely. The words sounded filthy.

"Just me and my rocks. No tools, no tape measures. Only a good eye."

"It's like hunting boys."

"Different medium. Same idea."

"That's true. If only the boys were as hard and docile as stones, life would be so much better." Brent sipped again from his coffee. Nick's silence was hard to read. "So, how do they stick together, these rocks? Don't you need cement so it doesn't all fall apart?"

"Anybody can build a wall with mortar," Nick said. "What skill is there in that?"

"None, I guess. Apparently."

"None," Nick confirmed forcefully. "That's the easy way out. The only mortar *I* use is balance. I don't even believe in breaking the rocks up with a chisel or altering their natural shape. I believe in taking what nature has given you and making it work, finding the right place for each stone."

"Sounds complicated."

"You just need to see it in all its dimensions at once, even the side that is not visible to you at any given time."

As Nick explained at greater length what was necessary for his craft, Brent stopped listening. He was enjoying too much the simple victory of having gotten Nick to talk. His voice was rich with his passion for his chosen work. He spoke intently, intelligently about what he was trying to do.

Brent was again surprised to find Nick was not as stupid as the stones he works with. Quite the contrary. He was laser smart, and peppered the conversation with quotes from poetry and references to jazz. At times, he got lyrical, using the words "persuade" and "dissuade" on the opposite ends of a pair of metrically balanced clauses.

From a purely sexual point of view, it might have been hotter, Brent thought, if he was big and dumb. But intelligence wasn't bad either.

What made Nick's talk particularly appealing was the utter loss of self-consciousness. He was entirely in the present. Somehow both oblivious to his body, but totally inhabiting it at the same time. He stopped to scratch himself, to twist a bit and get a crack out of his back, to crouch to lift a stone. Every movement was thoughtless, graceful, beautiful, the effort unconscious as if he was drawing the stone up into his arms rather than lifting it.

Brent guessed that people rarely asked Nick about his work. *Fools*, Brent thought. *The quickest way to a man's heart is flattery. Followed closely by teasing.*

Nick could have his balance, Brent decided. Flattery and teasing were all the mortar Brent needed.

"Need help?"

"No."

"How about that one?" Brent suggested. "That one there that has fallen off to the side."

"This one?" Nick peered at the boulder Brent had suggested, and then looked at Brent as if he had no eyes to speak of. "That one looks like it's meant for the bone pile."

"The bone pile?"

"That's what you call it when a farmer dumps all the rock when he's done clearing a field. Refuse. Excess. Stuff you're not using right now."

"Oh." Brent re-examined the stone. "No, I don't think that's bone pile material."

"No? Well, then, where should I put it, do you think, Mr. Sawyer?"

Brent had not really thought about where to put it. *Just pile it on the next one,* he thought. *What does it matter? Why do people always make such a big damn deal out of their passions? It's just piling rocks up, after all, I've been doing it since I was three years old.*

He kept these thoughts to himself. Instead, he got up and made a show of inspecting the wall, all the while rubbing his chin thoughtfully, like a professor of philosophy.

"How about here, doctor?" he finally suggested.

Nick shook his head and said, "It won't work."

"How do you know it won't work? You haven't even tried."

"I don't have to try. I can see it from here. Trust me, it won't fit."

"Yes, it will!"

The caffeine had kicked in. Brent was suddenly filled with words and conviction as he explained forcefully why the spot he chose was absolutely perfect. Nick stared at Brent while he explained, a Mona Lisa smile on his face that was absolutely inscrutable and would have given pause to anyone less jacked up than Brent was at that moment.

Then, while Brent was still explaining why the stone he had chosen was so perfect for the place he had picked out, Nick lifted the boulder in question and, in one swift movement, placed it where Brent suggested.

It looked ugly and teetered, unable to find a comfortable home among its brethren.

Brent stopped talking. He could not stand that Nick had won.

"You did that on purpose," he accused. He scrambled up from his sitting position and attempted to force the stone into place on the wall.

The stone proved much, much heavier than it had appeared in Nick's hands. Brent had to put nearly all his weight behind it to budge it an inch. And when he did so, he nearly dislodged all the other stones that Nick had set.

The uncooperative stone rolled off the pile and came to rest at Brent's feet, as if the stone itself could not stand the ignominy and embarrassment of being set in the wrong place.

Brent looked up at Nick. "I guess I should shut up."

Nick laughed. "Not as easy at it looks, eh?"

Brent kicked at the offending stone. "Damn thing's useless. You should throw it out. It's totally useless. A waste of good carbon matter."

"Not useless. It just looks useless when it's sitting on its own like that. Doing no work. But put it next to another stone, side by side.... then you have a wall."

Nick lifted the stone again. "Every one has its place, even this one. Even if it's place is the bone pile."

He surveyed a stretch of the wall he had built thus far that morning. Moving down a few paces, he fit the stone in where it belonged.

"It'll stay there a hundred years," Nick boasted.

"You're good."

"Thank you. I'm not bad. Not *all* bad."

"Whaddya call this, what you do?"

"This work? With weathered fieldstone? It's called dry-laying."

"Dry-laying?!!!"

Brent was unexpectedly delighted with the name. With all its multiplicitous, naughty possibilities. He offered to serve as Nick's apprentice any time. "I like dry-laying," he announced, drawling, provocatively cocking his body at the hips.

"It's hard work."

"Oh, I like it hard. The harder the better."

Nick smiled. Brent felt an unexpected, almost juvenile delight in having won this smile from the normally stern handsome face. Nick's mood was good today and the double-entendres seemed to please him rather than annoy him. Here, at work, it was all about the rhythm of stones. They revealed a surprising peace to his nature, a depth and stillness that Brent had not imagined.

"You should smile more often," Brent proposed.

"Maybe I should."

They stuck to safe topics—more about the stones, something

of Brent's work as a dancer. Nick surprised him. His knowledge of dance was limited, but his questions were intelligent and thoughtful. He seemed genuinely curious. If the stones were heavy, Nick's mind was light and agile. He never seemed to tire, working through the whole discussion, punctuating each point with the "ker-chunk" of stone into its rightful place.

Brent felt listened to. Closely listened to, more than anyone had ever listened to him. Brent was used to people who only gave him half an ear—city people, his family. It was his own fault, really, because he *did* talk a fair amount.

But Nick listened to it all, and he listened closely, to every word and nuance. And the result was frightening. Brent was not sure he wanted to be listened to so closely. Nick caught him on each lapse in logic and each bit of lazy thinking. But, at the same time, he sympathized with a depth of feeling that was startling.

I *really* could get used to this, Brent thought, sipping the dregs of his coffee in the sun while someone else did the work. *All I need is a cabin boy in a grass skirt fanning me with a palm frond.*

As the day wore on, a raft of thick clouds scudding in from the northeast swallowed the morning sun. They seemed to build up directly overhead as if there was some invisible dam in the sky they could not see.

The only sign that Nick was aware of them was an infinitesimal increase in the pace of his work. By late afternoon, Mrs. Sawyer, too, had become aware of the clouds. She called out to Brent to ask him to go down to the lake house and make sure it was closed up properly.

"There's news of bad storms coming," she said. "Thundershowers. Hail. Maybe a tornado." She spoke without worry, the tone of a woman who had seen all manner of New England weather and would trust the preparations she had made to see her through, this time, like the last. And soon enough, the sun would again shine. "Take my car. Only be careful, it's been acting up lately." She smiled at Nick. "As you well know."

"I'll go down with you," Nick offered. "We can take my truck if you like."

Brent was surprised by the offer. He would have thought that Nick would be reluctant to leave off work. Before Nick could change his mind, Brent quickly accepted.

When she went back inside, Nick raised his eyebrow. "Lake house?" he asked.

"Yeah. Her summer camp. It's on Sabbaday Lake. We grew up there. Before my Dad died, we spent all summer on the lake."

The camp was a rudimentary cabin. It had few improvements and no insulation, and little had changed since Brent's grandmother built it. Braided rugs covered rough-hewn pine boards. A wood stove hooked into a stone chimney. The fireplace was surrounded by soft, dilapidated furniture, and the cupboards were full of jars of pickled beets and the black-gold of mustard pickles.

Every available inch of shelf space was filled with pottery owls and granite inchworms and brass boats in full sail and wire butterflies alighting in a mason jar on a twig made of glass. There was a brass lamp fashioned to look like an old water pump and the prints on the walls were swampy woodland birds. On the wall between the brackets where fishing poles hung, a plastic Wal-Mart bass had been mounted. When you pressed a button on its gills, it flapped its tail and sang "Dirty Water."

"This is one of my favorite places in the world," Brent said as they turned in the long unmarked logging road that led from the highway to the lake's edge. "I used to sneak away here for days and have fantasies of kissing boys all by myself."

"We've arrived," he murmured.

Nick's head turned like an owl's.

"Arrived? Where?"

Brent pointed across the lake, where the storm clouds had gathered full and black. The lake was ominously still.

"When I was a kid, my best friend lived across there," he said. "In one of those houses. Which we used to call the rich people's houses." Brent laughed. "We had no idea what rich meant. Some better off than others, but none of us rich. His name was Bobby."

"The one I saw at the coffee shop?"

"That's the one." Brent was startled that Nick would remember or notice. "For a while, he used to come across the lake at night to see me."

They let the shutters down over the plate glass windows, and stowed the plastic yard furniture underneath the camp in the crawl space there. Pulled the canoe up over the pine needles and tipped it over so that it did not catch rain. Nick seemed to have an instinct for knowing what needed to be done without being told.

They had nearly finished when the storm hit. It came with a railroad noise. The wind upturned everything, shattering the lake's calm surface. The rain came down so hard it was like being peppered by marbles. They bolted for the camp, getting in under the roof in a matter of seconds, and yet still soaked to the bone. The shirt was clinging to Nick's chest, and his nipples had hardened in the chill the storm brought on.

Despite the damp outside, Brent's mouth went dry. He swallowed hard, trying to choke down the rising desire. The camp seemed suddenly tiny. Too small for the two of them.

He turned away. He made a show of looking out the window at the storm. Rain lashed down. The docks came loose from pilings. Boats dragged their moorings and a pair of canoes from the camp up lake shot down the shoreline like spears.

Brent ached for Nick to touch him. For the touch of his full lips teasing Brent's neck, Brent's ears. He imagined bending his head in submission to the thousand kisses. He imagined Nick's massive hands, rough but not unkind moving down over his shoulders, flattening over his belly, skirting the belt loops on his pants. He pictured the thrust of him from behind, the insistence of that massive frame, the hungry man smell of him permeating all Brent's pores.

Nick was still as one of the walls he had built. Brent wondered whether he even felt the impulse. Whether he had merely reined it in, or was oblivious to this powerful pull. His gaze was beyond Brent, out at the lake and storm.

How can he not feel it? How could he not know what Brent was thinking? The air was choking. The camp was turning colors around them. *How could he not be aware?*

The wind howled, and the neighbor's chimney gave way with a grating, wrenching sound, and it toppled down on the side of Mrs. Sawyer's camp. The kitchen cabinets burst open and shattered glass all around them. A branch crashed down on the porch outside.

Brent clutched at Nick. He half-expected the camp's wall to come down.

Nick seized him, grip tight, hands shaking, as if torn between the desire to thrust him away and the desire to take him in.

Brent forgot entirely about the wind and rain and damage. He felt only Nick's touch everywhere on his body, a hundred firebrands.

Brent broke Nick's grip with a quick upward stroke of his arms, and he proceeded to tear Nick's shirt off his body. It was soaked and fell to the floor with a satisfying thwack. Brent turned his attention to Nick's trousers, unbuckling the thick leather belt.

"I am not normally like this," Nick tried to explain. He was looking down at his loose belt helplessly.

"I am!" Brent spouted. "I'm a bitch on wheels."

Nick did not seem to know how to get his hands around this response. Brent stepped back, stretched his arms and revealed a patch of bare hip, abdomen. It captured Nick's gaze. Obliterated his thought. As Brent had known it would.

Nick babbled and lost his place. Looked away.

"I get mixed up when I talk to you," he said. "It doesn't come out right."

They shared a long, disturbing look. The broken glass underfoot made a sound like beach sand.

Brent tore off his shirt. Nick's eyes widened. He fell silent. His whole body seemed to grow in size as if the blood had rushed everywhere all at once. Nick's pants had flopped to mid-thigh and his cock bulged through his boxers, out through the flap, the tip of it red and swollen, a drip or precum on the end, glistening, even in the low and shrouded light.

Nick reached down. He nearly lifted Brent off his feet, as if he were just a stone he needed to fit where the place was right. He was eager. He pulled Brent against him, his hips thrusting against Brent's frame with bruising impact. Shots like a boxer.

Brent felt his hardness, the massive rude organ. Nick took one step forward through the litter of broken dishes. He braced Brent against the camp's doorframe and again he thrust up against Brent's body, crushing the breath out of him.

When he let Brent go, Brent slid downward, back to the wall, as if he had no strength in his legs. And then he was down on his back on the hard floor, his shoulder blades bruised. He looked up and Nick crouched over his face. Nick's powerful haunches were above him.

Brent ran his finger down the crease in Nick's ass, pulled aside his cheeks. They were firm and muscular. He slid his tongue into the place he had been invited. He worked down the crack, to the round puckered flesh. He worked his tongue in, forcefully, so that Nick driven upward by the surprise or a spark of electricity, as if Brent's tongue were a live wire.

I am going to reacquaint this guy with his asshole, Brent vowed. And then he settled into his work, wriggling slightly over the hard floor. Nick lowered his ass over Brent's face as if he would suffocate him with it. Brent felt his tongue actually inside Nick, along the walls of flesh. He used his teeth to knead the tiny puckered folds of flesh, to draw them away from one another, stretch them out. He tongued hard at the base of Nick's shaft, used his finger to slick through the wet, up in the ass. He probed and made room for the tongue. He felt the delicious assy stank on his face, on his cheeks and tongue, felt the few stray hairs and the weight of Nick balanced on Brent's tongue so that he felt like a gay Atlas, like he was holding up the whole world.

Nick began to masturbate himself. Brent tongued harder. In

time. He felt the helpless spasmodic jerks, the shaft grow more taut, the butt-wriggle more desperate. The strokes hard, and convulsive, the voice raspy and low and from another world: "ohyeah, ohyeah, ohyeah, ohYEAH!", Nick cried out. And then the drops of hot spunk spilled on Brent's chest, molten lava, hot solder, fusing them.

As quickly as he had begun, Nick released Brent. He turned away, snatched up his pants and his shirt from the floor in one smooth move. He buckled his trousers and beelined for the door.

He stopped, halfway out. His eyes were cloudy, the rain pelted his face.

"I forgot," he said, breathlessly. "The children. The children are alone up at the Lady Blanche house. They must be afraid of what might happen."

Brent nodded automatically.

As if Brent had given him some kind of permission, Nick darted out the door. Brent watched him leap from the porch to the ground without touching the steps.

Brent felt abused, mussed. He did not move for a moment. Then he gathered himself up from the floor. His breath came back to him, but his hard-on would not go away. He wiped the jizz from his body.

Then Brent heard the truck's engine roar, and the gravel crunch under the tires.

"Hey! Hey!"

Brent threw on his clothes. He ran outside and pounded on the door panel.

The truck skidded to a stop. Nick looked up, startled, as if he had entirely forgotten Brent was here. As if he did not remember who Brent was.

Brent yanked the door open. He shouted: "You brought me here, remember? You've got to give me a ride home."

"Get in!" Nick ground the truck into first gear. It began moving before Brent had a chance to vault himself through the open door. Gravel shot out from the tires.

They bounced and careened over the pitted road. Nick drove

grimly. The rain fell steadily. Both of them were shirtless. The road raced by.

Brent studied Nick. He did not know whether to be angry or not. Dusk had fallen by the time they reached the road to the Lady Blanche house. There was no light to be seen. The few streetlights they had passed on the way were without power, and the Lady Blanche house itself was a looming dark shadow. In the crashes of lightning, it appeared haunted.

They found the three children huddled in the library, away from the windows. A branch had fallen and broken a window and the rain was coming in. They were terrified. They threw themselves into Nick's embrace, teeth chattering in fear, and the body of the tiniest quaking, as he blubbered silently.

"Why didn't you go into another room, where the window was not broken and it was warmer?" Nick asked.

"You told us to stay here."

Nick nodded, but his eyes were looking elsewhere. His preternatural hearing had detected a broken gutter. He released the children, who did not want to be released, and bounded up the stairs two at a time.

Brent shouted up the stairs, proposing that they take the children home first and then deal with what was wrong with the house.

"You left them alone?" he asked. "Where's their mother?"

Nick appeared at the top of the stairs. A flashlight had appeared in his hand. His face was invisible in the dark, but his body revealed his uncertainty. He wavered, short little half-gestures cut off before fruition.

Brent realized: Nick does not want me to see Una, or Una to see me.

"She's away," Nick said somberly. Brent was certain he was lying. Thunder again crashed outside and tree branches scraped on the window glass. He was about to call Nick on his bullshit, but the children gathered around Brent's feet as if he could provide them shelter from the storm. There were more important things in this world than calling out a liar.

"Then they can come with me," he proposed. "My mother has a generator. They'll be safe and warm. And there'll be light."

Brent carried the children one at a time through the rain to the pickup, making them comfortable in the flip seat, until all three were snug under a blanket.

"Are we going to see Mommy?"

"No. But I've got the next best thing," Brent said. "We're going to see *my* Mommy."

This news was not what they had hoped for, and yet there was a definite spark of curiosity in them, as they had obviously not stopped to consider the possibility that Brent had a Mommy.

They waited in the steady downpour for Nick. From time to time, they saw a light flashing in a window of the Lady Blanche, first here, then there, as if he were searching for leaks.

"I'll be right back," Brent said. "Two seconds, I promise."

They bit their lips to keep from crying.

Brent rushed in. He tripped in the dark over some scraps of wood and cursed aloud. He stopped where he was before he plunged again through some construction boobytrap. What a stupid place, he thought, to leave children!

"Nick! Nick!"

"What?"

"We need to get those kids safe. We need to go. You can come back later."

Grimly, he mentioned the leaking gutter.

"Never mind that…the kids…"

"You take them," he proposed, "and come back for me."

"You sure?"

"Sure, I'm sure. What does it matter? You're better with them than I would be. And I have to fix…" He stopped when he saw Brent's skeptical look. "Division of labor," he explained.

"They need you."

"Not me. They need somebody. A father. Which is…" he

stared at Brent with mute appeal, and then decided against finishing his sentence. He rarely gave in to speaking his self-pity aloud. "You take 'em," he said roughly.

Brent did not bother to argue. He piloted the pickup to his mother's house, driving over the grass to bring them right to the door. Mrs. Sawyer fussed over the children, fetching them dry clothes to change into and brewing up cocoa. The youngest was exhausted, and maybe a little feverish. She supplied him with a blanket and ordered Brent to set a fire.

Once they had settled themselves and gotten food in their bellies, the younger child slept. Mrs. Sawyer played games with the oldest two. When the children began to tire—to say nothing of Mrs. Sawyer—Brent took over and began telling camp stories to the oldest.

"Don't you scare them now, so they can't sleep, Brent Sawyer!"

"These kids? These kids are the bravest in the world. You should have seen them up there at the Lady Blanche house. They're not going to be afraid of a silly story."

He looked to them for confirmation and they nodded solemnly. Proudly. They had not thought of themselves as brave.

Brent had entirely—maybe deliberately—forgotten about Nick. It was much later, long after the ghost stories had been concluded, that Nick's knock came on the door. He had walked three and a half miles through the steady rain.

He waved off Brent's apologies.

"Don't worry about it. Took me longer than I thought in the dark. Kids in bed?"

"Yup."

"Thank you for taking care of them."

"No problem. It was a pleasure." And so it had been. Whatever Brent might think of Una, she had raised her children well. "You must be cold."

Nick shrugged. He was still in the wet T-shirt he had been wearing earlier in the day. His muscles bulged through the taut fabric. He looked heroic. Invincible. This was the guy you wanted on your side in a fight.

"Can I go up to check on them?"

"OK. My mother just put them down a half hour ago, they might still be awake."

Nick sat on the edge of the bed and roughly mussed the children's hair.

"You're all OK, right?"

They nodded wide-eyed.

"You weren't scared were you?"

In unison, they shook their heads, so eager were they to please him.

When they returned to the living room, Adam was slumped in a chair chatting with his mother.

"Electricity's out everywhere," Adam was saying. "The town's pitch-black."

Nick's appearance in the doorway made Adam go silent. He looked up at him with wide, respectful eyes. Then he looked at Brent, back to Nick, smiled mischievously and happily.

"What're you lookin' at, punk?" Brent asked. "You met Nick?"

"Not officially," Nick said. He offered a hand, which Adam shook warily. While the others talked of the storm and storms like it, Adam's eyes kept jumping toward Nick, appraising him from head to foot.

Finally, he got the courage to speak. "Were you ever a professional athlete?"

"I never liked organized sports."

This answer brought a palpable disappointment to Adam's face.

"You don't do sports?" he asked skeptically.

"Organized sports. I do other things for fun." Nick thrilled Adam with an hour of tales of mountain climbing, triathlons, and kayaking. "I don't need to measure myself against others; I test my own limits."

Adam was impressed, and ready to join Nick on his next great adventure.

"If you want," Nick said, "I'll take you along." His eyes shifted to Mrs. Sawyer. "If your mother lets you."

"We'll see," said Mrs. Sawyer, and then proposed to leave "the boys" alone for the night.

"You'll set up Nick with a place to sleep?" Brent suggested.

"He can have my room" Adam volunteered. "I'll sleep on the couch."

Nick said he would go back to the Lady Blanche house.

"You'll do nothing of the sort!" Mrs. Sawyer declared. "I won't let you. And there's the kids to think about, waking up in a strange house."

"OK," Nick agreed, "You're right. But no one should be put out because of me. I'll sleep on the couch." He glanced up toward the open door of the guest room at the top of the stairs. "I should let them know where I am in case they get scared."

Mrs. Sawyer smiled approvingly. While Nick was on that chore, she commented that he would become a wonderful father— sooner or later.

"Husband?" Adam asked scornfully and shot a hard look at Brent. He seemed to think his mother was very old-fashioned.

Brent thought: *Not if I can help it. Or at least, not a wonderful husband. Not to Una. He can do all the fathering he wants. Just no husbanding.*

Adam was positively glowing with excitement at the prospect of going on a trip with him.

"And you'll come, too!" he said to Brent.

Mrs. Sawyer met Brent's eyes with a murderous look. "Don't you encourage him!"

"We'll see," Brent said in a singsong imitation of his mother that made them all laugh.

When Nick returned from the children's room, Adam challenged Nick to an arm wrestling match. The match last all of two seconds.

"Aren't you going to let him win, you bully?" Brent asked.

Adam looked insulted. Nick looked scornful.

Nick said, "Hell, no, give him a couple of years and we'll be likely to break even. Got to get my wins in now."

Adam glowed. Nothing could have pleased him more than the prophecy of his future strength from somebody who looked like he might know a thing or two about strength.

As Adam got ready for bed, he cornered Brent and whispered enthusiastically, "*That's* the kind of guy you ought to marry."

"Not very likely," Brent said in a normal tone of voice. He caught Nick's eye over Adam's shoulder. *Does he think about that ever? Does he ever imagine what it would be like for us to be together?*

Nick's craggy, stony face revealed no answers. After Adam crashed, they stayed up late, sitting at opposite ends of the sofa. They talked about everything under the sun. They were hard, long conversations. They disagreed about everything. Which delighted Brent. He had never met someone so thoroughly contrary to himself.

But they were both avoiding something. Both avoiding that powerful magnetism that made it feel like they had to cling to the armrests to avoiding being drawn together. This obvious topic of conversation was like a third diner at the table, which they were trying to ignore in hopes it would go away.

Outside, the storm had not yet given up its fury. The wind howled. The old house was full of drafts, and wet streaks marked the windows. Brent offered Nick the pullout cot, set up in his room. Or in Adam's. Nick refused the offer.

"The couch," he insisted, "is fine with me. That way the kids know I'm here, remember?"

He sat on the sofa's edge and began to unlace his boots.

For a long moment, Brent stood at the door. The first boot came off, then the second, then the socks. Then Nick looked up at him. Mutely. Maybe appealing.

He peeled off his shirt. He was watching Brent watching. Absolutely deadpan. Calm.

It felt like a test. Brent was churning like the storm outside.

"Good night," he said, but he didn't leave.

Nick slid beneath the blanket provided. He pulled it to his chin. And then, abruptly, Nick turned away.

"Good night," he said.

In his bed, Brent tossed and turned. His mind raced. He thought of nothing but the feel of Nick's body earlier that day. Pressed against him at camp. Rutting hard.

There were bruises on Brent's backside where he had been jammed against the doorframe. His skin branded wherever Nick had touched him. His muscles were pleasantly sore. His joints wrenched.

His heart wrenched. Yes, his heart.

This cannot go on, Brent thought. *We cannot keep seeing each other.*

Brent had never been with anyone who could get such a rise out of him time and time again. He did not understand this attraction that was well beyond physical, into another dimension. And with a man he hardly knew.

He touched himself, but it was not enough.

Brent slipped out of bed. The clock read 11:15. He had been in bed just fifteen minutes, although it had seemed like an eternity.

He looked at himself in the mirror, full-length naked. Lithe powerful shoulders and thighs from years of training. Body fat low. Waist trim. His frame was boyish and narrow—as hard as he might try, he would never be a muscle man.

He pulled on a pair of athletic shorts. Again, he consulted the mirror. *Still,* he thought, *I look good enough to eat.*

He pulled down on the pants so the waistband was over the mound of hair on his pubes. His buttocks exposed on the backside.

I still could pass for a teenage boy, he thought, pleased. He stood on his toes to tighten the muscles of his butt. He flattened out his stomach, and pumped up his arms.

Then Brent thought suddenly: *I should be more discreet.*

He pulled on a tank top and turned this way and that in the mirror.

120

Still too much come on, he decided.

He located a sweat shirt. Then flannel pajama bottoms. The only skin he was showing now was hands, feet, and face. Heart pounding, Brent slipped downstairs.

Nick was face up, his eyes open, the blanket now pulled down to his waist.

"Aren't you a little warm?" Nick asked. He did not seem surprised to see him.

"Um, well..."

"Modesty" Nick guessed.

Brent blushed.

"Don't worry," Nick promised, "I won't attack you under your mother's roof."

I should not have come back, Brent thought. *Damn this guy's confidence. Damn his arrogance. I should go back upstairs right now and put him in his place.*

Instead, he sat on the edge of couch near Nick's feet.

"How disappointing," he said, coquettishly.

"Do you enjoy being attacked?"

"A boy's got to have a hobby." Brent bit the end of his thumb.

He shed the sweatshirt. Time slowed. The minutes were drawling and languorous. Brent yawned and stretched and shed another piece of clothing.

He looked at the fire. Rain fell outside. With the windows shut, the room became stuffy and Brent shed more clothing. He was down now to his tanktop. He felt Nick's eyes search his shoulders, trace the muscles. He felt hot, and a little sweaty.

Then, like water flowing toward gravity, he was drawn into that solid embrace. Nick's lips were wet and full. He kissed Brent deeply. He pulled at his lips, bit them gently between his teeth. Hours seemed to pass before Brent breathed again.

"Did you like that?" Nick asked.

Brent nodded.

"It's been...forever .. since I kissed anybody."

Brent nodded. Wide-eyed. Wishing Nick would kiss him again.

"Well, then, you've got some making up to do."

Brent reached behind Nick's head and pulled him again close. His hand ran greedily over Nick's chest. Nick's hand in turn made for his waistband. The tank-top came off.

Nick found the smoothness of Brent's torso. Brent breathed in, inflating his chest against that hand, firming the abdominals for Nick's touch. The hand found the waistband again.

Brent drew his breath in yet further, until he was dizzy. The concavity of his belly gave permission for the hand to pass beneath.

But Nick did not take it. He seemed content to kiss, sleepily, and stroke Brent's hard cock through the flannel pants.

Brent arched. He let his neck be kissed. He let his throat be kissed. He let his little birdlike collarbones be kissed.

He wanted to be kissed everywhere by this man. To be touched everywhere with these strong hands that seemed to be making, firming, forming his body, as if Brent were nothing but raw clay.

Finally, the stroking hand got tired just when Brent was on the edge of climax. Nick slept a heavy contented sleep.

And somehow Brent was glad of it, even if he would not get to sleep for hours. He did not want to lose this warm feeling in the cold of post-orgasmic depression. He did not want to be the first to get off.

Another night. It would have to be another night. That was what Brent promised himself. And he was pleased with the promise. All of a sudden, he had a future with this man. Maybe not long. Maybe not forever. But a future.

Nick's face was an inch from Brent's. Brent breathed in his breaths, one after another, regular as a clock.

I could lie here forever, Brent thought. *Breathing the air he so lately breathed.*

This fascinating man. This intolerable man. This arrogant, beautiful man. Brent wanted to lash him, lovingly. To call him names, endearingly.

Nick slept.

There would be nothing, he thought, *Nick and I ever agreed on. We are so very different.*

And yet his body fit into Nick's like a stone that had found it's place and some work to do. Hours later, still in Nick's grasp, reluctantly, sweetly, Brent surrendered the long moment to drowsiness, and he slept.

***

When Brent woke, morning sunlight had broken through the open window. The clouds were gone and the day already had a hazy cast that promised it would be a scorcher.

Brent closed his eyes. He remembered where he was. He reached out his hand to the hard body beside him. He felt the reassuringly even rise and fall of his massive rib cage. Brent purred contentedly.

Then he heard a stifled giggle. He popped open his eyelids. Standing on the steps in a little row were Una's three children. They were laughing and covering their mouths and poking each other's ribs with their elbows.

Brent's eyes went wide. He poked Nick, who was instantly awake. He looked at Brent with uncomprehending eyes, as if he were no more than a morning apparition that would disappear in good time, with a cup of good coffee and a clear head.

Brent jerked his head toward the kids. Nick still would not look.

And then one of the children, the oldest, asked aloud, "Nick, why is Mr. Sawyer in YOUR bed?"

Nick leaped to vertical in one explosive movement, dumping Brent unceremoniously to the floor. He hurriedly buttoned his pants, which Brent did not remember having worked open.

"Mr. Sawyer and I were talking. He fell asleep there, by mistake," Nick said bluntly. Then he added, unnecessarily and untruthfully, "I slept on the floor."

A quizzical expression crossed over the child's face. The

children's looked at one another and raised their eyebrows, but no one asked for any further clarification. They had long since stopped trying to understand the odd ways of grownups.

"Smooth," Brent said once the children had been ushered to the kitchen by Mrs. Sawyer for a rousing breakfast.

Nick looked at him murderously. He was pacing like a wild cat in a zoo.

"What on earth were you thinking of," he finally hissed, "falling asleep there? It's...criminal. They're just young kids."

"You didn't seem to mind so much last night."

Nick spluttered and could not find words for his frustration.

Brent supplied them: "Last night when you kissed me."

"You threw yourself at me."

"Like a cheap hussy," Brent agreed. "Which you like."

Nick's voice boomed: "I do NOT LIKE THAT. CATEGORICALLY NO. NEVER."

The happy breakfast sounds from the kitchen stopped. There was silence, and then Mrs. Sawyer's heels on the linoleum floor. She pushed open the pantry door.

"Would you boys like something to eat?"

Her voice contained a dire warning. Her eyes flashed like the lightning from the night before. Submissively, Brent and Nick joined everyone in the kitchen.

The kids were loaded in the pickup and Mrs. Sawyer had waved her goodbyes and gone inside. Nick was hustling to get around to the driver's side.

"Are we going to talk about this, Nick?"

A pained expression crossed Nick's face.

"About what?"

"Last night. Yesterday."

Nick shrugged, obtusely as if he did not understand.

"The sex," Brent added bluntly.

"That wasn't sex."

"What was it?"

"Fooling around."

"Whatever. Are we going to talk about it?"

"What's to talk about? It's one of those unfortunate things."

"Unfortunate?" Brent was stung. He felt the color appear on his cheek.

"Unfortunate," Nick said firmly. "I have my life together, all planned out. I've found someone I can be with. Someone who shares the same ideals and values," he added significantly.

"Not like me."

"Not like you."

Brent stood between Nick and the door of the pickup. Nick looked at him now, directly at him. Bullying almost.

Brent yielded the door.

"What difference does it make to you?" Nick asked irritably. "You do this all the time."

"What?"

"Tease, fool around, whatever. Just one more notch in your..." Nick could not seem to come up with an appropriate comparison. And this fact only increased his irritation. "There's nothing to talk about," he snarled. "What I have with Una makes a few kisses insignificant."

Brent stepped back as if he had been slapped.

"You can't deny that–"

"–that I find you attractive? So what? I'm not a kid anymore, I don't have to follow the pull of my dick."

"It's more than that and you know it."

"*It is not more than that.* Your problem is that you've confused sex with a higher calling." He opened the truck door. "Say goodbye to Mr. Sawyer, kids."

"**Goodbye Mr. Sawyer!**" the kids sang out, abashed and without enthusiasm. Nick drove off.

CHAPTER 12

The children were mercifully silent and well-behaved. They filed into the Lady Blanche house like a set of tin soldiers. The power had returned and there was nothing to be afraid of any more.

Without a word to them, Nick set to work repairing the broken window in the Library. He fetched a stool and pulled down the plastic sheeting he had spread over it during the storm. Swept up the mess of glass, wet, and splintered wood at his feet. Carefully, Nick plucked shards of broken glass from the frame and dropped them into a bucket.

But his mind was elsewhere.

He had behaved badly, and he knew it. His mind replayed Brent's pretty, wounded face. The genuine hurt in Brent's face had come as a complete surprise. Nick had really convinced himself that Brent did not have any feelings. That he did not care. That Brent was all about sensuality and sexuality and surface and nothing more.

It unnerved him that Brent had feelings. Feelings for *him*. It set a kind of panic to his heart, like a gerbil spinning on a wheel.

He should have been kinder. He should have explained to Brent that he had no choice. Or that he had already made his choice.

But he had panicked. Worried that the whole wall would come tumbling down from this stupid mistake. Worried that Una would find out and would doubt him. Worried that he had given the children a reason to doubt him.

He glanced back at them. They were watching him, wide-eyed. Two of them were sitting cross-legged in the arched entryway to the library on the unfinished floor. One of the children had fetched the broom and was holding it at the ready.

Glenda the Good Witch, Nick thought. He was lucky to have so much. *How could he have been so dumb, as to threaten it?*

He turned his attention back to the shattered window. Sleeping in Brent's arms hadn't seemed dumb at the time. Not last night, in the warm bath of firelight. It had been all Nick had wanted. All he had been able to think of, and damn the consequences. It had been the kind of moment that knows no tomorrow and no yesterday, but only the rich well of contentedness you find sometimes, rarely, when you are least looking for it.

Nothing else had existed for Nick last night but the shape of Brent's shoulders, the fineness of the bones of his face, the way he crumpled to laughter and his teeth flashed. Nothing but the stubborn positions he staked out in opposition to Nick's own, more conservative views. Nothing but the funny stories from the dancing stage, which seemed almost cartoonish to Nick, who lived everyday working in the very real.

He's not real, Nick told himself. *Brent is not real.* He was just a dancing flame. All the boys pretended to be good. All of them loved you for a little while. They did not know the meaning of devotion, of permanence, of—

"Damn!"

Nick had cut himself, a silver sliver of pain on the edge of glass that did not look so sharp. He swore again, the children jumped, and he felt the damp trickle down his finger.

He held it in the sunlight coming through the window. The blood was bright, fresh, full of oxygen.

One of the children exclaimed, "You're bleeding!"

Nick nodded dumbly. Blood roses bloomed on the floor. He climbed down from the stool, and twisted a paper towel around the wound.

"It's fine," he said. He mustered a smile. "Really. It's fine. The bleeding has stopped."

She looked at him as if she wanted to believe him, but could not be sure.

Nick felt a wave of tenderness. He knelt next to her and scooped her in. Sometimes the right choice was not easy. Some things were worth fighting for. He wanted to build a castle wall around her and protect her from doubt and treachery.

Una would soon come home again. She had been angry and had gone to do some thinking on her own. But she would soon be home. For her children. And for him.

You can love someone in spite of his or her flaws, he thought. This fact continued to amaze him. He thought of his father, whom Nick had learned to love. Would he put Una through the same things his mother went through? Would he force her to make the same killing compromise?

Nick breathed the name on his lips: Brent!

I cannot love him, he thought. I already love someone.

He held the little girl tight and they both looked out the empty window frame of the Lady Blanche house into the bright morning. The grasshoppers called out and the sun beat down and the mountain meadows around him seemed to go on forever.

***

After breakfast, Brent retreated to the backyard. He was sitting on the portion of the wall Nick had built, feet off the ground and kicking like a little kid. The wall was not finished—just a couple more feet remained. A couple of hours' work.

Brent jiggled a bunch of gravel in his palm as if it were pennies. Idly, he began to reproduce Nick's wall in miniature on top of the wall next to him. He balanced the little bits of gravel one on another, until he had built a wall on the wall.

Those bits of gravel that didn't balance well, he tossed aside into the mud puddle from last night's storm. Instantly, he regretted throwing them away. Nick's wise words echoed in Brent's head: Everything has a place.

And a time, thought Brent. A place *and* a time.

He was a dancer. Timing was everything. And in a duet, most clearly of all. You could not let down your partner. Brent hastily swept the stones back into his palm.

Brent thought: *I could make Nick happy.*

The screen door banged open. Brent looked up quickly, as if a prayer had been answered and Nick had turned back.

But it was Bobby. He was looking a little hangdog. And maybe some hungover.

"Jeez," he said. "We drank a lot the other night, didn't we?"

Brent's nerves were on edge. The night at the clock-fest seemed a hundred years ago, a flea on an elephant's ass. He could barely muster the patience necessary to put up with Bobby, who—Brent guessed—had probably come for absolution for his sexual sins.

"Not so much."

"Well, *I* did."

Reluctantly, Brent gave him what he was looking for: "Yeah, you seemed drunker than me," he acknowledged.

"Oh, I was," Bobby said quickly, seizing the opening. "Hammered. Blitzed. Sometimes I do dumb things when I'm drunk. And say dumb things, too." He flashed his dazzling movie-star smile, and then it again disappeared. "But you know that."

Brent gave a wry smile. "I guess I might have seen it from time to time over the years."

There was an awkward silence. When Bobby spoke, his voice was so small Brent could hardly hear him.

"I thought maybe...maybe...I kissed you."

"Might have happened once or twice."

"Oh. I see." Bobby fell silent, but his mouth was working furiously.

"What?"

"Well.... I just didn't want.... Didn't want you to get the wrong idea," he mumbled. "You know..."

Bobby kicked the gravel at his feet and drew patterns in it with his toes. Brent let him stew.

"Like before!" Bobby blurted. "I mean, when we were in school."

It was the first time Bobby had ever referenced their having had sex back then. Brent was stunned. For many years, he hadn't even been sure that Bobby had not conveniently blocked it out.

"I didn't mean for you to get hurt back then. I was just a horny kid, and I really, really liked you, I did, but-"

"Bobby!" Brent said sharply.

Bobby looked up, wide-eyed.

"Yes?"

"It's OK. Not a big deal. Not then, not now. I'm not under the slightest impression that you are or were in love with me."

Brent watched Bobby turn this idea over in his head.

Brent sighed. "Or that you're gay. OK?"

Bobby smiled sheepishly. These had been the words he had been seeking.

Brent frowned. He was tired of making other men happy. Telling them what they wanted to hear. Fuck that. He was going to go off somewhere and become a hermit, where he didn't have to deal with another one of these selfish narcissi who could not grow up.

Bobby quickly hid the cheer from his face. He said, "Not that you're not hot, Brent. I mean, I wish I had a body like you."

"Enough!" Brent growled.

"No, really. I mean it."

Bobby put his hand on Brent's shoulder, but when Mrs. Sawyer leaned out to ask if she could fetch them some lemonade, he leaped away as if Brent were a live electric current.

After Mrs. Sawyer retreated inside, they stared at one another like a pair of strangers.

"You'd be surprised," Brent said. "Some guys—even gay guys—don't think it's so lucky. To sleep with me, I mean."

Bobby frowned. "What?"

"Nothing. Drop it."

He looked away, looked at the wall Nick had built. After a while, he turned back.

"Still here?"

Bobby nodded, wide-eyed.

"So, is that what you came over to make sure, that I didn't fall in love with you again?"

"Um, no, actually." He started to say something. Then stopped. "Are you OK, Brent?"

"I'm fine."

"Boy trouble?"

"You were saying why you came?"

"Oh, yeah. Well. I just wanted to ask if you would take over my parents' house while I'm away. I got to go away for a few days."

"Sure. Of course I will. Where you going?"

"Going to chase down the wife," he said.

"I thought you were broken up for good?"

"Well, I called her up yesterday. I thought we'd patch up. Give it another try. You know how it goes."

Brent shook his head. He knew. The cynical part of him said that Bobby had been so terrified of being gay that he had gone running back to his marriage to hide.

"Good," Brent said. "You *should* go back."

Bobby looked pleased. "I should? You think so?"

"Oh, yeah, definitely. You guys are in love. Always were. That's special."

Bobby was visibly relieved. Thrilled. Buoyant. He was pleased that he had this special love that somebody like Brent had noticed. That made it real. Which was good enough for now to bank his future on.

As Bobby walked back to his car, Brent wanted to plunk him on the ass with his handful of gravel. *Each one has its place,* he thought ruefully.

Brent counted himself lucky that Bobby had never been interested in Brent. What a disaster that might have been. Now if Nick had grown up in Holmstead County—*that* would have been the guy Brent would have had the crush on. Maybe Brent could have caught Nick before this whole idea of marriage had got in his head like a virulent cancer.

But Brent had been a different person then, when he had lived in Holmstead. A different person with different needs. Maybe even if Nick had been around back then, Brent would have chosen Bobby over Nick, as crazy as that choice seemed now. Maybe he had needed the infatuation and heartbreak of loving Bobby to know better.

People make the craziest choices, he thought. Love makes people do the craziest things.

CHAPTER 13

The letter that arrived in the mail was creamy and gilt-edged like a formal wedding announcement. Brent groaned when his mother handed it to him. He had had about enough of other people's weddings.

"It's not what you think," Mrs. Sawyer said.

The envelope was addressed to Brent and Mrs. Sawyer, and the card inside requested the pleasure of their company at a dinner in Bar Harbor, a coastal resort town an hour and a half away.

In careful architectural script at the bottom of the page, Nick had written a short note in longhand: In thanks for your kindness to our children.

Brent's mother immediately declared that she would not go.

"At my age," she said, "I have no business traipsing over half the state for a bite to eat."

Brent paced the kitchen. How incredibly awkward! Was Una really going to permit this to happen—for them to sit around a table in awkward silence with the—to Brent—obvious sexual charge between him and her husband-to-be like an unwanted guest?

It was merely a polite gesture, Brent decided. No one actually expected him to accept this invitation. It was a form of social lubrication that should not be taken seriously.

He again examined the card. The two handwritten names at the bottom of the invitation nauseated him.

"It must be nice to have an ampersand between your name and somebody else's, don't you think, Ma? It's like the adult equivalent of drawing a heart and a plus sign in seventh grade. Nick & Una," he scoffed. "Sounds like a personal injury law firm."

Mrs. Sawyer glared up at him. "Do you mind? I'm trying to write."

"Well, sorry. How many different ways are there to say no?"

"Many," she said firmly. "It's more difficult than saying 'yes'."

"Touché, woman. It's not so easy when you're a slut like me."

"Brent!"

"I'm *joking*, mother. Did we forget to take our funny pill this morning along with our geritol?"

Mrs. Sawyer quickly finished her draft, folded it up, and put it in a floral envelope.

"Couldn't you use something less girly, Ma?"

"I'm a girl."

"But I'm not."

"This note's not for you. It's my note."

"Yeah, but you can just sign me up at the bottom. You know, Mom-ampersand-Brent."

"If you would like to respond, Brent Sawyer, write your own. Like an adult."

"Mother!"

She looked up. "I want you to take responsibility for yourself," she said. And she kept her eyes riveted on his, so that he would not mistake her meaning.

"You think I should go?"

"I have no opinion one way or the other," she said. "But I think you should make the decision for yourself, whether you go or not, and you should follow through on it. Like an adult. And not waver back and forth like a child."

Shit or get off the pot, Brent thought. It was what his father would have said in the same circumstances. His Mom was a little more civilized. A little more floral, in fact.

"OK, Ma, I'll do it," he said enthusiastically. "Right this very minute."

But he did not do it. Brent put off his reply for several days, each day meaning to send a note saying that he could not come. He decided that the moment Nick showed up to finish Mrs. Sawyer's wall, he would tell him. For four days, at seven a.m., Brent perched on the porch with a cup of hot coffee and a sense of complete determination, and waited for Nick. Who did not appear.

The day before the day the dinner was scheduled, the doorbell rang.

"May I come in?"

It was Una. Her hair was long and straight, two hundred strokes every night while her children watched. Her make-was up tasteful and reserved, careful not to destroy the milky purity of her Irish skin. It was, Brent decided, really very fine skin, admirable in a woman her age, with three children behind her.

Brent, who was dressed in a pair of ratty at-home lounging shorts made of corduroy felt distinctly at a disadvantage. He had not done his hair. Or showered. Or applied even the least drop of beauty products. On the way to the porch, he managed to steal a wet hand of water from the bathroom sink and spike up his bangs at least.

What in God's name was she doing here?

She came right to the point.

"Nick is a very good person," she began.

Brent nodded.

"Nick feels he has certain...obligations. He takes them on, heedless of the cost to himself."

"Amen," Brent said.

She said, "That's why, when you brought our children here the night of the storm, Nick felt he owed you something."

"Oh, it was nothing," Brent said quickly. "We were glad to help out."

"I know," Una responded. "I know it was nothing. I told him as much. There were a hundred places you could have brought the children."

"Um, I guess."

"And yet you brought them here. Knowing Nick would have to follow."

"Well, I brought them here because—"

"Never mind," she interrupted. "It doesn't matter. The fact is, he feels he owes you something and insists on this dinner invitation, no matter what I say."

"Yes." Brent said. "Least he could do, I guess, for a pair of strangers rescuing his children—your children—and keeping them safe, warm, and entertained for hours."

"Look," she said. "Let me get to the point. You'll decline, right?"

"Actually," Brent replied in tones equally direct and icy, "I was looking forward to going to dinner with Nick."

"You're shameless."

"I like to think so."

Her mouth pursed into a mask of hatred so pure and desperate that Brent actually drew back in his seat. Her milky skin went crimson.

"The way you've thrown yourself at Nick is really...despicable. Totally undignified."

Her finger stabbed the air repeatedly.

"He...does...not...want...you." She said it slowly, emphasizing each word, as if Brent were an imbecile, who needed the obvious spelled out in capital letters and underlined. "That part of his life is over."

"The gay part, you mean?"

"Nick loves me."

"I don't doubt it. But *you* don't love him."

She glanced down at her shoes.

"He gets what he wants out of it," she murmured.

"And you get a green card."

"Not everything is as crass as you imagine. A girl has got to protect herself. No one else will."

"You're afraid."

"I'm no such thing."

"You are. You think you're going to lose him. You're worried you've already lost him."

Two circles of color appeared on her pale Una cheeks like a couple of bull's-eyes.

"You're impossible!" she raged. A nasty Irish curse dropped off her lip, like guano from a bird. "You're just a failed has-been, looking for somewhere to curl up and die!"

The remark stung, and she saw it had hit its mark.

"I know all about it, Nick told me. He told me how pathetic you were, washed up at—how old are you—thirty-four, five..."

"Two. Thirty-two."

"How self-defeating you are. What a loser. A quitter. Afraid of success. Sabotage your own career. Nick told me all about it."

"You should leave now," Brent said.

"Are you coming to dinner?"

"I am."

"You *will* regret this."

"Do you need to be shown the way out?"

"I can make my way on my own, thank you."

"I hope I never get like you," Brent said.

After the door slammed, Brent glanced up to see that his mother, Mrs. Sawyer, and his sister Heidi had come into the room.

"So you're going to accept the invitation? You're going to dinner with them?" Heidi asked.

Brent felt suddenly shy.

"Pigheadedness," Heidi said quietly, "is not a virtue."

She shared a quick and knowing look with their mother.

"Uh-oh," Brent said. "Now don't start stirring at the cauldron again, ladies. It's just a dinner, right?"

Neither woman responded. They did not need to respond. It was much more than a dinner. It was a showdown.

Brent sighed.

"Look, Heidi, Mom, there's a part of me that hopes he does not give up this scheme with Una. A man who knows what he wants, and sets out to get it, and won't be turned aside...there's something fantastically beautiful about that. It's rare. And admirable. I wouldn't have a problem with that. God speed, I say. Go meet your destiny."

Brent stood like a mock soldier, gave a firm little salute, and began to play taps through a horn he fashioned from his hand.

"Oh, bullshit!" Heidi said, unable to keep the smile off her face. "You're playing to win, I know you too well, brother of mine."

Their mother sighed, shook her head, and dropped into a chair.

Heidi looked at her guiltily and then said, "OK, OK, if you can't beat 'em, join 'em. Let's see what you've got stashed in your closet. At least we'll make you look pretty."

When they looked at the finished product in the mirror, Brent could not suppress a smile.

"I'd do that guy," he said cheerfully.

"You'd do lots of guys!" Heidi frowned at their reflection in the mirror.

"What?"

"Brent, I wish you'd at least admit...."

"Admit that I've fallen in love with Nick?"

"You said it, not me."

"I haven't."

Heidi's face fell.

"And don't even start giving me lectures about denial," he warned. He glanced at their mother. "We'll leave that to Mom."

Mrs. Sawyer said, "No, I'm happy for you. Happy you're doing what you think is right."

"I do think it's right. I really do."

"OK," she said. "I'm only afraid you might be disappointed in the results."

"You think Nick can't be persuaded? Loved?"

"Every man has some weakness, Brent. And Nick might not be strong enough to realize that he needs you."

"You really think he needs me, Ma?" Brent was shocked by her words. And wanted desperately to believe them.

She reached out and adjusted his collar.

"I do," she said firmly. "I do think he needs you. And he would be lucky to get you."

Brent hugged her fiercely.

CHAPTER 14

The next day, the day of the dinner, Brent shed any residual misgivings. He again donned the outfit he had chosen for the occasion and looked at himself in the mirror. He was pleased with the reflection. Heidi would be proud, he thought.

Nick had left him a message, instructing Brent to meet him out at the Lady Blanche house and proposing they all drive to Bar Harbor together. He explained that he was now working feverishly after work to complete the house by the promised deadline, and was sleeping there every night so as not lose even a spare hour.

When he pulled up, Nick was waiting in the doorway. He was dressed in a light summer sweater and he slung his sport jacket into the back seat.

The tidy, stylish clothing only enhanced his rugged beauty, and Brent was suddenly shy. He nudged the car into gear and headed back down the long driveway.

"To Una's house?" he proposed, putting more cheer into his voice than the prospect deserved.

"What for?"

"Isn't she…?"

"She won't be joining us."

The words were somber and final and did not invite any further questions.

Accordingly, Brent could not resist asking, "Couldn't get a sitter?"

Nick smiled grimly. "I thought," he suggested, "that before we started for Bar Harbor, I would show you some of my work. If you want to see it. Our reservations aren't until nine."

SCOTT & SCOTT

"Sure," Brent said. "I'd like that." Who was he to be worried about Una's behavior?

For the next two hours, Nick took Brent on a tour of Holmstead County. They stopped at a half dozen houses and passed by with only the slightest reference at least that many other specimens of Nick's stonework.

It was magnificent work. At times, absolutely breathtaking. At one farm in particular, built as a country retreat for someone from the city, Brent was amazed by Nick's handiwork. It had never occurred to him that a four hundred foot stone wall could appear light and complex, a twist in it like DNA, so that gradually what had been the bottom of the wall became its side, and the side became the top, twisting over the landscape. An arch over an entryway in the meadow, with a slatted gate on a hinge, became a stone footbridge over a good sized river, where it seemed to tremble in the dappled sunlight reflected off the surface of the river, but it was as sturdy underfoot as the earth itself. This was art—a careful selection of stones to put together, a judging of slopes and angles.

"Nick, you're brilliant."

Nick smiled demurely, murmured thanks, pleased it seemed just to bask for a moment in the presence of his handiwork. It was obviously a kind of moment he did not often permit himself.

At some of the places they stopped, the property owner joined them. Invariably, the owners were friendly, full of respect. They shook Nick's hand warmly and clapped him on the back. Often, they mistook Brent for a customer, and would—without prompting—extol Nick's talents and work and sometimes—before Nick cut them short—his honesty.

Each time his former clients made this mistake, Nick firmly corrected the impression. He introduced Brent as his friend, not a prospective client.

And each time, without blinking an eye or reflecting any doubt at all, the owner would say 'good to meet you' and shake Brent's hand equally warmly. Any friend of Nick's was a friend of theirs.

This must be great to be taken so seriously, Brent thought. In his life, he had always to prove himself before winning respect. He was too small, too gay, and on top of it all, a dancer. People thought of him as lightweight—morally, physically, emotionally—until he proved otherwise.

But Nick—people seemed to detect something sturdy in him from the first glance. Something they could rely on. They trusted him.

Brent had never been to the Bar Harbor restaurant Nick had chosen. It was in a Victorian inn right on the water on the quiet side of town. They were supplied a table on the porch. The twilight had set in, and the lightest of ocean breezes was like a whispered kiss. Candles flickered in hurricane lamps. Behind them, a jetty made of square cut granite boulders curled out around a protected harbor belonging to the Inn; a half-dozen sailboats were moored at close quarters.

It was a spot designed expressly for romance. The thought made Brent's heart thud, and when his cocktail arrived, he downed half of it to steady his nerves. He felt embarrassed at being here, as if they should be in some giant steakhouse with cigars and port and a raft of homophobes, a place more suited to doing business or a formal occasion with a comparative stranger.

Seeking a release from this awkward realization, the impending panic that made him feel like an imposter, like they were both imposters playing a great big game of make believe, Brent pointed at the jetty that reached out into the water and protected them from the open water.

"Is that your work, too?" Brent asked. He wondered whether Nick, too, regretted this choice, this selection of table, this particular flickering candle, each of which demanded some performance from them that they could not—or did not want to give. It was as uncomfortable for Brent as a blind date with someone you knew in the very first moment of meeting that you would never in a million years be attracted to.

Nick looked up from his study of the menu, a study as intent as if he were looking at ancient scrolls.

He glanced out to the water, spotted the jetty, and the haunting, questioning look left his face. Again he smiled. His eyes were soft as if he had just woken, but the angles of his face were made starker by the candles flickering shadow and the low light.

"Sometimes," he said self-depreciatingly, "I let other people have some fun."

Nick smiled. Brent smiled.

"Come on," he teased. "You should have pretended you built it just to impress me. It's very unflattering."

"I thought you were already impressed."

Brent felt the color flood his face.

"I would never lie to impress someone."

"I was joking," Brent said. He wondered silently: *Are there other reasons you would lie?*

"I know." Nick returned to his study of the menu. "But I'm not."

A hollow whistle hooted from the bay. A line of buoys lit with red and yellow lights led beyond the jetty and into the water. Brent did not open his menu. He simply stared at Nick.

Are you a unicorn? Or just a humorless asshole?

When the waiter came to take their order, Brent was flustered and unprepared, but neither Nick nor the waiter paid him the slightest notice. Nick knew his way around the menu and the wine list, and he ordered for both of them.

Brent found that he actually did not mind submitting his appetite to Nick's care and control.

His role was not to question the sumptuous restaurant, the table for two, the fabulous array of appetizers and entrees that he would have to spend a week in the gym to work off. His role was not to question Nick's motives or assumptions or identity.

Brent was only there to go along for the ride. *Be in the moment,* he thought.

"Wasn't it nice," he asked, "that all your customers regarded me as an honorary straight man?"

Nick laughed out loud.

"What? Why are you laughing?"

"No offense, sweetheart-"

"Sweetheart!"

"-but I don't think many people would mistake you for straight."

Brent flushed, not because he had any notion that he was 'straight-acting', but because he was so delighted—flattered even—that Nick was teasing him. He pretended an outrage he did not have, listing all the manly and wonderful accomplishments he had achieved, from kissing girls to fixing sinks and—once—even watching Nascar.

There was laughter in Nick's eyes, and his shoulders relaxed. They bantered back and forth, and sipped at the sweet Riesling that accompanied the appetizer of mussels and andouille sausage. A fresh green fragrance rose up from the herbs scattered on the steaming plates.

Nick breathed deeply, appreciatively. His eyes ran over the food like a pair of greedy hands over a naked body. He looked up at Brent. Happily.

"Isn't this great? I come here at least twice per year," Nick said, "to get my fill of the finer things." He plucked a mussel from the platter between them. "It's a tradition."

"Do you bring Una here?"

"No. I've always come alone."

Brent tried to picture Nick coming here alone, a couple times a year. He pictured the big white tablecloth with one place setting, the faraway eyes, the silence at the table amid the hum and chatter of the other guests. He pictured Nick sipping his wine and looking out into the harbor and the vast ocean beyond. The sound of buoys. The cry of gulls. The vast unending break of swells on the jetty.

It seemed unbearably sad and lonely and depressing. A lighthouse out on a point winking on and off, pretty but seldom visited.

"You look very handsome," Nick said.

"I thought you would think it was too slutty."

"Same difference," Nick said with a genuine laugh, appreciative and full, that made it feel like he had ransacked Brent's body. And taken everything he wanted. Several times. Hard.

Brent's mouth went dry.

"We shouldn't drink so much," Brent cautioned. "We have to drive home." He helped himself to another glass of wine.

"I've booked a room."

Brent froze. He was sure he had heard correctly. A room. Not rooms plural. Just one room. A room with a bed. Maybe double beds? Brent looked at the inn's authentic New England decor and thought it unlikely.

He swallowed hard. "A room?"

Nick nodded. His eyes were impassive. Brent wished he could see what was going on in that restless mind.

He sipped again from his drink and looked away. He hated his own indecision. He hated feeling as if he was always the one off-guard, whose footing had slipped. It was not like him. He felt like Nick believed he had made the move that marked his checkmate and Brent had not even known he was in the game.

And I don't even like this guy! Brent reminded himself.

It was a patent lie. He felt Nick's legs shift under the table, an inadvertent brush on his shins.

And he felt, for no good reason, that Nick longed equally to touch him.

They were in a staring contest now. Eyes locked. Still Nick was not bullying, not aggressive. If there had been a challenge in his remark it no longer resided in his eyes. Instead, his eyes were a promise, a pledge. It would have made as much sense to question his motives as to question the motivations of a stone. Or the swelling ocean.

Twilight had given way to night. A tray passed, and Brent smelled aromas of roasted chicken, warm bread, currants, pine nuts, oil and vinegar. Brent leaned over the table, reached out, and drew a finger on the slender edge of glass of the hurricane lamp. It was hot to the touch, but he did not draw away.

They both watched his finger trace its way around the lamp, first close to Nick, and then to himself, and then close to Nick again. On the third pass, Nick reached and stopped him. He lifted Brent's finger away from the glass and said, huskily, "You're going to burn yourself."

There was no more sense in asking where this night was going. Nick's hand touching Brent's burned more than a thousand lamps. Brent knew where he would sleep that night. And he did not want to ask about other nights. He squeezed them out from his thoughts.

Pay later, he thought. *Play now, pay later.*

For the rest of the dinner, they said hardly anything more. They clinked glasses, they shared food. They stared at one another across a table that suddenly seemed too wide.

They lingered after dinner and did not feel hurry. The moment drew out to its full length, like a cat outstretched in a patch of sun. Hands resting on their glasses brushed against one another. Other tables cleared out. Fewer sounds passed over the open water and the candle burned low in the glass.

Brent was happy to linger. He felt displayed, as if Nick wanted everyone to see the man he was bringing to bed. To show Brent off.

Brent imagined what other people were seeing: this handsome, happy giant paired with himself. He saw himself at the table and imagined he looked ripe and cute, slim, fetching.

He felt like royalty. A crown jewel. Wanted in every way, desired, cared for. Loved.

A voice in his head howled in protest: To bed? Love? Was he crazy? A matter of days ago he had hated him. A matter of days before that and he had not known him from Adam.

Brent said to that voice: It must begin somewhere. Every journey must begin somewhere. And in love, for love to last, it must begin here with this, it would need much more over time, but this was the minimum, this undeniable, unfathomable attraction, could not stop looking, could not stop touching, could not stop thinking.

Brent suffered a rush of thoughts, a surge of desire, that wound around one another until they were indistinguishable. Love. Bed.

Crazy. Yes. No. Maybe. Who ever knew anyhow? No decision was without risk. If you insisted on being certain, the time would pass you by, the clock strike, and the chance lost.

The time was now.

As if he had reached the same conclusion, Nick asked, "Shall we?"

They mounted the hotel's grand stairs with Brent in front. He walked stiffly, both because of tipsiness and because he was sure of the hungry eyes on his butt and would not have been surprised to feel the nip of Nick's teeth.

Keep walking, he told himself. Nick opened the door to their room with the key, and held it open above Brent's head. He ushered Brent under that bough-like arm.

Because of Nick's upward reach, the cropped sweater he was wearing pulled away from his belt buckle. Beneath the lower hem, a trail of fur showed over a hard flat belly that was like a boy's in everything but muscle.

The door shut behind him, plunging Brent in sudden darkness. The lights snapped on, and Nick's giant arms closed around Brent like the jaws of a steel trap.

Brent closed his eyes. Then opened them again. It was a beautiful room, outfitted in gorgeous antiquities, but he saw none of it.

He felt the tightness of arms on his chest from behind and could not breathe. His heart thudded, his crotch grew hard. He smelled the man close to him, the already familiar smell he had smelled at dinner. He felt the hot breath on his neck. He felt small and protected in the shelter of this man, and he had an overwhelming desire to be devoured, stronger than any he had felt.

Brent pressed his buttocks back against the hard frame behind him. Nick was bent at the hip to accommodate the difference in height. Nasty thoughts of being taken rudely and anonymously and against his will from behind gave way to a different fantasy.

Nick propelled him toward the little balcony beyond the sliding doors. There was just enough room for a breakfast table and two chairs. The balcony overlooked the harbor. Stars streaked the night.

Nick pressed Brent against the rail, the weight of his huge frame crushing Brent to nothingness. He murmured in his ear. Brent's arms were pinned to his side.

The words that reached Brent's brain were sweet nothings, animal sounds that might simply have been kisses, all utterance indistinct. And yet Brent thought he understood this language, had always understood it from the moment of his birth.

Brent crooked his neck into those teasing lips as they touched a searing nerve that seemed to run right down his body. He swiveled in Nick's arms, like a turn-style, until his back was to the sea, the top of the rail to his back, and—finally—Brent was facing Nick.

Brent looked up into his face. He found the lips that spoke so well in that private, ancient language. Brent took those with his own. He gently bit them, pulled on them, covered them with his own.

He felt a deep, confirming breath well up in Nick. Nick shuddered, as if he had just shed a second skin.

Brent felt Nick's hardness through his summer-weight trousers. It was another shock. Another surprise. Like the first time you ever touch a boy and feel him respond to you, the culmination of all your hopes.

Nick's hands gathered and linked under Brent's ass. There was a powerful upward surge. Nick drove back, pinning Brent on the high railing of the porch. At the same time, he put his tongue deep into Brent's mouth.

Brent felt like a pincushion, as if he had been penetrated many places simultaneously. He felt a curious lightness, a floating, more so than at any time that he had danced.

He sucked on the tongue, arms around Nick. The delicious sense of vertigo from being on the top of the rail only added to his thrill.

He kissed hungrily, devouring stone's face, letting the scruff of his shadow rip up his face like a pumice stone. He kissed his neck, ran his hands through Nick's thick hair.

Then Nick snatched him away. He carried Brent easily, hardly a strain in his muscles, as if he weighed nothing at all, an inconsequential burden.

Brent clung to him, impeding his steps. Stone stumbled. They wrestled around the rooming, banging into furniture and yanking bed spreads in knotted fingers, bruise to bruise—on the lips, on the back, fingers in the butt.

I'm going to be a mess, he thought. Brent never had been afraid to have it rough, but had never before done it with someone this big. He felt everything. Absolutely every fire of touch.

Somehow the slightest edge of pain could add clarity and sharpness to everything else you were feeling if you truly surrendered yourself to it.

Nick slung him down on the edge of the bed.

"Everything," he said, "has a place."

Then Nick backed toward an armchair. His eyes never left Brent, as if he could hardly believe he existed or was afraid he would escape. He guided himself to the chair with a hand, and sat back, his legs splayed wide, his hands in his crotch, stroking and teasing his own manhood through the thin linen trousers.

Brent made a move to get off the bed to approach his lover, but Nick waved him off.

"Take off you clothes!" he ordered. His voice was almost harsh, a laceration, as if he had been whipped.

Brent began to take off his clothes. He felt unaccountably shy. Almost fearful. He had not felt before this combo of eagerness and shyness, and it made him almost forget how to undo his buttons.

As his shirt came off, he heard murmurs of appreciation from deep in Nick's throat. Again, in that heady, naughty language they both spoke.

When Brent's pants dropped, he thought he heard Nick gasp. Brent ran his hand over his skin, arched back, over to the side, as if he were stretching, slowly, sensually, in some amazing, sensual dance to a music only he could hear. He was wearing only the smallest, light blue pair of bikini briefs that his cock had tented to tautness.

Unable to restrain himself any longer, Nick jumped forward with that characteristic alacrity, as a lion might dive on its pray. He moved impossibly fast for a man of that size.

He dropped to his knees at Brent's feet. He kissed Brent's belly, put his tongue in his navel, kissed his way down through the electric spots in the crease of Brent's crotch.

Then, slowly, he drew down Brent's underwear and let his hardness spring out.

Nick gave a little yelp of joy, or surprise, or both, as if it was more than he had ever wished come true.

Nick's face was filled with adorable wonder of a little boy. He kissed the tip of Brent's penis, and Brent's eyes filled with tears at this tender gesture. Nick kissed Brent's strong thighs, moving down to the knee, and using his hands to bring the underwear to his ankle.

Brent flinched, but Nick kissed the thin scar at the edge of his knee that had spelled the end of his career. Kissed it twice.

Brent nearly wept at the kindness, as if all the frustration that scar had brought was being drawn out through this man's lips, like poison from a snakebite. He half-expected the scar to disappear.

He stepped out of the underwear, which Nick swept away. He took the giant's hand. He tugged him down to the bed on top of him. Brent rolled back so that his legs went over his head so he was looking through the V of legs at Nick standing above his bum, staring down at it like a man possessed, reaching out like a man who did not think it could really be there for him.

Nick undressed, his hips pressed up against Brent's butt, leaned slightly forward to support Brent's pose. His hands brushed Brent's buttocks as they removed his trousers. He let loose an appreciative and hungry sigh.

Brent watched him. He could not tear his eyes away.

Nick was magnificent. Chiseled shoulders, tanned to the waist, pecs, and hard nipples, narrow waist, and abs that Brent made Brent's hands itch to run over them. Black hair, well-tamed on the chest, but not shaven. Thighs defined but not too thick, the quad muscle quivering, and ample hardness under the white boxers sticking straight out between them.

Nick, in turn, could hardly look at Brent. His eyes scurried away, and came back again and again. Brent knew he looked good from the naked need in Nick's eyes.

Nick kicked off the last frustrating pantleg, and then reached over and snapped off the light before he peeled off his underwear.

Brent was touched by this gesture of shyness. But when he felt Nick's burning member against him, pulsing and hot, as if they had fallen asleep with embers from a glowing campfire up against his skin, he thought maybe Nick had done it for Brent's sake, so that he would not have time to get scared at the size of his penis.

Brent closed his hand around Nick's penis, and placed it against his butt, in the crease, felt it slide back and forth looking for an opening. In the dark, every patch of his skin seemed alive, taking in sensations that Nick gave him. Fed him. Braised him.

He heard the tearing of foil, felt the trickle of lube, the stretch of a condom over hard skin.

Nick's thick fingers worked Brent's ass. Opening it. Pleasuring it with small circles that widened and stretched him.

Brent wanted those fingers in there, inside him. Deep within his being. He felt the rough calluses on bare skin.

Brent opened his mouth to pant in delighted joy, and immediately his mouth was filled with more fingers from the other hand, which he bit and sucked on. He felt the sudden bend over him, the bed giving way beneath him with the extra weight. Rough lips clasped over him. Nick's weight pressed down, bending Brent's legs almost behind his head, ankles around his ears, stretching Brent like a piece of salt-water taffy. Yoga never felt this good.

The fingers kneaded his flesh, found an opening, slipped inside him and out.

Then the unbearable and delightful happened, inevitably, as he knew it would. That unmistakable largest finger pressed into him, through the narrow ring of his sphincter.

Brent cried out at first, his body rebelling, bucking. And yet his body wanted it, was hungry for it, even if he felt awkward and virginal, as if his experience were limited.

Nick relaxed, eased up. Brent began to apologize, but Nick shushed him with a finger to the lips. He was gentle, but insistent. He said, "Shhhhh" and Brent's whole body obediently responded. He relaxed and Nick's cock was then somehow deeper in him. Slowly, slowly. Back and forth, just an inch at a time, the control a magnificent knife-edge. Brent let all resistance go.

Nick sensed it, and released that edge of control. He had needs to satisfy. His hands were steel traps. He wedged Brent hard, spread his legs wider apart. The gentleness turned into firmness. Brent gaped wide, until he thought he could go no wider. And yet Brent wanted more of Nick in there, in his ass, wanted his whole body. And then there was more in, and Brent felt Nick's scrotum slapping up on his ass. He swore he could feel the pubic hairs. The ring of his rectum was stretched in a fire of something that might have been pleasure, or might have been pain. He did not know. He did not care.

Nick gripped Brent by the back of his bent-over thighs as if he could vault himself further in that way, his whole weight behind his cock. His hips drove his cock as hard as a drill. Brent felt a dull ache inside him, every nerve ending was alive.

Nick fucked him and fucked him, and it lasted forever. There was no time.

Nick's murmurs and grunts went silent as he built up to a shattering climax. Brent felt Nick's whole body quake and quiver, and when Nick exploded in him, convulsive, hot, it was as if one of his stone walls came tumbling down on top of them, burying them in dust and rubble. Twice more Nick convulsed, and Brent was delighted joyful, thankful for the orgasm, for the experience, for the seed.

Nick withdrew carefully, rolled over and collapsed on the bed, his arm around Brent's chest and Brent's legs still encircling him, Brent's hips turned to the side. He shuddered there with aftershock. Took great heaving breaths.

It was Brent's turn. Brent mounted him, rutting against the man's chest with his cock. Against the hard abdomen, pressing down on him until—only second later, he spewed all over Nick's chest and collarbones and neck.

Nick gave a final grunt of approval, tipped his head back to enjoy the warm shower.

"I love that," he said, or rather groaned. His hands had come to Brent's two hips, gripping him tight as if he wished to fix him there forever.

CHAPTER 15

It wasn't until they were cleaned up and Nick was sleeping, that great body spent, that Brent's thought strayed from that room, that bed, this body between his legs, that hot skin brushed up against his own, the smell of spunk and sweat cloying and delicious.

Even now, an hour later, Brent's skin was alive with sensations, present and moments past, little sparks and fireflies. He felt pounded, good, sore, deliciously used and grateful. He had sensed—even entered—the openness in the man. He had gone right into the pit of Nick's heart, into the wound and the passion.

Brent thought: *in this one night I have seen more of him than any man. I knew my way around. I belong here. Before I met him, I knew him better than Una.*

This conviction should have been a comfort to Brent. It should have made his night.

But, paradoxically, it did not. As the sounds of the inn died down for the night, and the streets grew quiet, and he could hear more clearly the lap of the ocean, doubt spilled into Brent's thoughts like chill in the night air, a damp sea breeze through the door they had failed to close behind them in the hurry of their lust.

I already know him better than anyone, Brent thought. But would this change anything? Do anything? Make any difference in the world?

Brent now knew Nick well enough to know the stubbornness in the man. The determination. And Brent knew Nick had given his word, not just to Una, but to the children, and because he had given his word, there would be no going back. Brent knew this. He knew it for certain.

Nick would not admit a bad decision; what mattered more to him than anything in the world was his word. And Brent did not for a moment think that a few moments in bed would change that. However hot. However disturbing. However explosive.

Nick was a better man than that.

Brent shivered. His leg and chest were exposed. He heard the mournful lowing of buoys on the unstill water and hoot of a horn that signaled a bank of fog somewhere had come in.

Brent slipped from the bed. His left leg was nearly asleep from the weight of Nick's body. He limped to the bathroom and gathered a robe around himself from the back of the door.

The robe was woman-sized, and short. Brent looked at himself in the mirror. His face was flushed, looked honest, almost naive.

You're being a fool, he told his reflection. *You've made a mistake. You've fallen in love.*

In the cool after midnight, Brent was embarrassed that he had given in. He had been a fool to think this would change anything. Deep down, he suspected himself of secretly harboring hope for a wedding band and box of chocolate hearts on his pillow.

Nick was not the kind of man you changed. You only endured him for as long as you could. He was made of stone. He would not wear away.

Brent flicked off the bathroom light and returned to the bedroom. He gathered himself up in a wicker chair, feet off the floor, arms circling his knees. He made himself small and watched the sleeping giant.

Even now at his most slack, Nick's body was firm and tight. His sleep was without disturbance. *The sleep of the just,* as Mrs. Sawyer would say. *The sleep of the righteous.*

Brent could barely restrain himself from shaking Nick awake, shouting and screaming, prying from him each and every mystery until he had none. So he would know. Now. For sure.

Brent tightened his grip on his own knees, shrugging further back into the chair's embrace. He had a deepening sense that when

Nick woke, the world would be changed. Irrevocably. Nick would not love Brent in the morning. That was certain.

Or, if Nick loved him, he would never allow himself to express it. Which amounted to the same thing. The same tragedy.

They had had this one night together. This one point in time.

Brent sighed. He was already nostalgic for this one night. He would have to treasure it, because—Brent told himself—he would not get another.

Brent tried to be firm with himself. To force his inner being to accept and understand this truth, which he knew as certainly as he knew his name. *This is it. This is the one night. Make the moment last. It is all you will have, Brent Sawyer.*

Nick stirred in his sleep, and panic shot through Brent. He shrank into the chair as if, were he not seen, Nick would not wake. Or would not realize what he was stirring and thus would again fall sleep.

Nick's arm flung out suddenly. It moved over the bed like a man reading Braille, and then settled into place. A minute passed. Again, Nick was still.

It would have been easy to believe that that outstretched arm had been reaching for him, unconsciously seeking Brent in the dark. How pretty that would have been. How perfect.

Moonlight filled the room, a silver glow of intense light. And then, moments later, it was gone, the moon having risen over the trees and the roof's overhang.

Love was like that, Brent thought. A moment that was soon gone.

And how stupid you felt afterward, when you looked back, and interpreted an involuntary movement of muscle, a mere electric impulse, as if it had something to do with you.

Love sucks, Brent thought. And again he was flooded with the shame of having given in. For not holding out for a deeper promise. A longer promise. Silver. Gold.

Brent fingered his asshole under the terry cloth. He felt

the places on his body Nick had touched. They felt purpled and bruised.

Indeed, Brent felt all-over bruised. Sore. Tender. It was not so much a physical sensation as an emotional or spiritual sense. As if he had exposed some delicate part of himself to wear and tear, the part of himself that should be kept hidden. Protected from rough handling.

This vulnerability made Brent want to flee now, to go back. Not just to Holmstead County, but all the way back to the City. Immediately. This very moment. Before the sun rises. In the City he never let down his guard. In the city he did not allow himself to be vulnerable.

He looked again at the handsome form sleeping on the bed. The hard flesh draped with sheet.

Unattainable men. Why on earth was he always throwing himself at unattainable men?

Of course, he could attain him. He could go over to the bed, rouse him, bring him to orgasm, ride his cock until Nick exploded up into him. Would he find it at some vulnerable point other than orgasm? Not likely. Not ever.

Nick probably had one expectation of him: that Brent would eventually leave Holmstead County, and things in Nick's life would get uncomplicated again.

The afterglow had deserted Brent's body entirely. He felt desolate. Emptied of sensation.

It could be so much different, Brent thought. What a pair they would make if Nick would let it happen. There was joy to be had. Nick knew it as well as Brent.

But Nick would squander that chance. That was the maddening thing: he would squander it in a heartbeat, out of fear of having his heart broken and out of some sense of maddening obligation to this woman and her children, an obligation he ought to have been able to meet in a hundred other ways than the one he had chosen.

Why did things always seem so obvious when you were on the

outside? How could a man who prided himself on his word be so insistent on a life of lying?

Brent felt as if he had touched on the key to Nick's mysteries. But it was 3AM. He was awake alone. No doubt it would all be forgotten by morning.

Brent unfolded his body from the armchair. He let the robe drop at his feet like a whisper. He stood naked in the sea breeze flowing through the open door to the porch. He felt naked to the core, naked beneath his skin, transparent.

Then he returned to Nick's bed. In sleep, Nick's body instinctively formed a protective cocoon around Brent. He accepted this protection, despite all the misgivings. He pressed himself into that wall of rock-hard flesh that Nick had created, and hid there like a child from monsters outside.

He vowed to leave in the morning before Nick woke. And because of this vow, he permitted himself this indulgence, the luxury of Nick's embrace, this little fantasy of happiness, love, and content.

No harm done, he thought. Or rather, no further harm than what had already been suffered.

***

By the time Brent again opened his eyes, the huge bed was empty. He lay still, eyes closed, listening hard. All he heard was the rustle of wind through paper. The sounds of the harbor were long into full swing. The sun was beating down so hard Brent swore he could hear the noise it made.

He opened his eyes and shifted his glance toward the mirror over the dresser. It reflected an empty room.

Brent sat bolt upright, astonished, filled with fiery outrage. How dare Nick leave him here in bed! How dare he abandon Brent like some cheap trick he had picked up in the back room of a dance club or some rain-dripped alley!

Brent threw off the covers and swung his feet to the floor. And then a teaspoon clinked on a platter, and the sea breeze lifted the long curtain over the door to the porch. The curtain billowed and beneath it Brent caught sight of a powerful calf muscle.

He heard a low chuckle that at first he thought was directed at him, but he realized it was something Nick had read in the Sunday paper that had made him laugh.

The view from the porch looked different by day, much harsher, as the sun reflected off the surface of the sea, blinding Brent. There was none of the velvet darkness and soft light of stars.

Nick was happily munching away on toast. He was reading the paper, stark naked. The rails of the porch were made of stone.

His coffee was black. Somehow an antique silver coffee service had materialized on the porch while Brent was sleeping.

He smiled broadly at Brent. A triumphant wolfish grin, Brent thought suspiciously. He drew the bedsheet more tightly around his body.

"Sit down. Coffee."

Both phrases were commands. Brent shifted toward a chair, but Nick pulled him down to his own lap and dandled Brent on his knee like a child.

"Don't fuck with me before I have my coffee," Brent muttered. He tried to pull away. He was not in the mood for being manhandled today. He braced himself to rise, but Nick's grip tightened on his hips.

"I love it when you talk tough," Nick said. He studied Brent a moment longer, as if he was daring Brent to fight to escape.

"Let go of me."

Nick released him.

Brent tied the sheets at the thin part of his waist, half a rump showing, angles down into his crotch, hip bones stretching a tight stomach he had had since he was thirteen and which, nearly twenty years later, hardly looked any different.

Nick scratched himself where Brent had been sitting. Nick's cock was already half hard and he was looking like he would like to see what Brent was hiding under his shroud.

Brent allowed him a peek through the long slit where the

edges of sheet bunched and did not overlap. He thought: *I am an inveterate tease. An unreconstructed, unrepentant bitch.*

He was not sure he liked this part of himself this morning.

Over coffee, they engaged in obligatory, desultory conversation. Nick praised the morning, and Brent scowled. Nick praised the brew, and Brent complained it was bitter before he had even had a sip. When he choked some coffee back, Brent burned himself and swore.

"Fuck. Fuck. Fuck," he said aloud and sipped the hot coffee he had spilled off his hand. He looked up. "So, we headed back now?"

"Soon as we have our breakfast." Nick leered. He had in mind a different kind of appetite.

"I don't need any breakfast. Just coffee."

He plunked his mug down for a refill.

They watched the sailboats leave the harbor. They heard cries from captains directed at their crews.

As if he was addressing the departing sailors, Brent said, "What happens when we get back?"

He blew on the coffee to cool it off. Little ripples crossed the brown surface and lapped on the other rim.

The silence grew too long. Nick, too, had been looking at the ocean. Color had touched his cheek.

"I've got to work today."

"And tonight?" Brent said it almost without interest. He was compelled to say it. It was from the script of a hundred bad tricks. He had no expectation of an answer that would mean eternal love, or even vague interest.

"Taking care of the kids," Nick answered.

"Of course."

Brent watched the movements of the facial muscles beneath Nick's skin. Brent stifled the urge to release him from his sense of obligation to speak or explain or promise. Why should he make it easy? The truth was out there in front of him. Let Nick confront it. Let Nick understand. If he were such a man, he would say the truth: That this woman and her children were not going to disappear.

That they were what Nick wanted. That Nick was deliberately and thoughtfully choosing them over Brent.

All the thrashing and interference in the world was not going to change it. Heidi had been right—Brent had been foolish to stick his nose in here where it was not wanted and where he was likely to get hurt. It was not his business, not his place.

"She would let me have you on the side, you know."

Brent blinked his eyes and cocked his head. He was not sure he had heard correctly. Was Nick offering him a place as his mistress?!!!

Nick laughed, amused by the surprise or outrage on Brent's face, a look he had expected and Brent had obliged him with.

"Just kidding," Nick said.

And yet, Brent thought he detected something under the laugh, some selfish impulse that Nick wished he could strike this bargain with Una. Because he believed Brent would certainly accept, as if some of Nick, some measly portion of his attention when he was horny or bored, was better than none at all.

Brent began to get ready to leave. He did not bother to shower. Pulled on a pair of jeans. Ran some stick over his pits.

A steady stream of invective broiled through his mind. He could feel Nick's eyes on him trying to avoid upsetting the balance.

In the bathroom mirror, Brent tried to make his hair obey but it would not. It was tufty and uneven, ruined by sleep.

Nick appeared over Brent's shoulder in the reflection in the mirror. Brent watched him raise his hand and set it on Brent's shoulder.

"I'm kidding," Nick said again.

Brent shrugged him off and continued to fix his hair. "No you weren't. But thanks for the offer. Very flattering."

Nick's face clouded. "I didn't make you any promises."

Brent turned to face him, so he would not have to see his own face, which looked blotchy and angry.

"Don't worry about it, OK? Your honor is intact. Your word.

162

I'm not going to sue you for paternity or false promises or whatever. I'm a big boy now."

Nick studied him, and Brent would have given anything to know what he was thinking. Probably judging whether he could trust Brent's words. Avoid a scene. Judging whether he would get away without having paid a cent for what he had taken.

He was caught entirely by surprise when Nick said, "I saw you dance."

"Yeah, you told me," Brent snapped. "Down at the Wang." He slipped away, underneath Nick's arm and began to ransack the bedclothes for his sweater. How stupid, he thought to have worn something so slutty, so nighttime. It would look ridiculous to be wearing it this morning on his way out to the car.

"No, I mean, your mother gave me one of your videos. I saw you dance. You were..." Nick seemed to lose his voice as he sought the word he wanted..."magnificent."

Brent held his sweater bunched in his hand. He was nonplused by the unexpected compliment.

Brent abruptly slipped the sweater over his head. He took one last long hard look at Nick.

"Thank you. I'll be down in the lobby."

The eyes of the other guests and the lobby staff searched for Brent's bags and when they realized he did not have any, knowing looks set in. The clothes did feel garish and wrong in the light of morning. They exposed the fact that he had unexpectedly spent the night and was leaving alone.

They know everything, Brent thought. *They are laughing at me. You idiot, they said. You went and fell in love.*

He felt cheap and tawdry. One of a hundred other whores. Red velvet and torn stockings and lipstick smeared over his face.

Brent abandoned the seat he had taken in the lobby, and went out to the steps. And from the steps it was a short walk to the car. And from the car, it was a short drive to the highway. And he went, dreamily, without thought, and it was only when the yellow lines were whizzing by on his left that he seemed to wake from these slow, graceful movements, and realize quite clearly that he was going to leave Nick behind.

He felt neither satisfaction nor elation nor any particular sadness. He was just driving, keeping the car on the road.

Getting distance, he told himself, getting perspective.

And so it surprised him to find the wetness on his face and the clouded vision of the highway ahead, as he realized with astonishment that he, Brent Sawyer, was crying.

CHAPTER 16

Somehow, it did not surprise Nick that Brent was gone. That the car was gone. It was like he had known the story's ending before anyone had finished telling it. The empty lobby, the empty parking space—they were familiar sights. Sights already seen. A familiar landmark after a hard drive.

He felt a small sense of relief. Wicked and shameful. But undeniable. He felt a great weight had lifted, as if he had pushed past some period of trial. Sun had broken. The witches of Salem had been put to death by piling rocks on them until their chests broke. Nick had felt the same way, but now a decision had been reached. Clear in his mind what the right path was. Burden lifted. No longer carrying around the weight of stones, of walls. The choice was right. Right for him. Right for everyone else.

He took a walk behind the hotel, along the docks and out toward the jetty. He won admiring looks from girls in bikinis on the docks. He won a haunted stolen look from some poor closeted man renting fishing tackle at the ship's chandler.

He stepped out on the jetty, walked to its very end. There seemed no hurry. Slow as an ocean. Inevitable. It was obvious now to Nick that he would do the right thing. He had obligations. This stolen night with Brent was not his proudest moment, but perhaps it was a necessary moment to put things in perspective.

The sun warmed his body. He peeled off his shirt. He felt the pleasure in his body, remembered the pleasure in Brent's body.

That customary wary, hunting feeling in his belly that he had carried around for years as if it was a part of himself was gone now. He felt smug and satisfied. I have overcome something, he thought. But what it was he could not be sure.

The view was clear over the ocean. To Ireland, he thought, I can see.

He felt frisky, and it was all he could do not to dive in to the ocean and wash himself clean.

At the front desk, they told him he had missed the early morning busses and that he would have to wait until noon for the next departure for Holmstead County.

Instead, Nick made his way out to the highway and put out a thumb. The first woman who picked him up was a harsh, chain-smoking motherly sort, who chewed him out for the danger of hitching, and then recalled her own hippie days.

Then there was a young landscaper in a pickup truck, who kept a bottle of Bourbon beneath the seat. He railed about the Democrats and the people from away and everyone who was not like him. When it was time for Nick to hop out, he became sentimental and gave Nick two chestnuts to remember the ride by.

The last ride was from a bookish, scholarly man, sixty or more, a used book store owner, who made no secret that he found Nick pretty, but his fawning came in a friendly, half-hearted, pleasant sort of way.

To each of them, Nick was unfailingly polite. He was soaring above them. When the bookstore owner spoke of art, Nick responded, but his mind was on a higher topic entirely. On truth.

There were still things to do. Things to arrange with Una. The woman with whom he shared so much in common. With whom he planned to spend a life.

He was ready finally to do right by her. All the rest could wait. He had all the time in the world to deal with other matters in his life. First things first.

Una was at the end of this ride, waiting for him.

He glanced at the used bookstore owner, who was talking fondly of skinny-dipping in his youth, and Nick had an impulse to tell him his secret.

He interrupted the bookstore owner's story.

"Have you ever heard of a dancer named Brent Sawyer?"

"Modern or ballet?"

"Modern."

He thought he had not, and so Nick described the dance, with a great pitch of enthusiasm, the words tumbling forth like water from a hydrant.

It was so unlike him to speak volumes, and to an unproven stranger, that after fifteen minutes he began to go hoarse.

"Good God," he said, "Would you listen to me, now, this diarrhea of the mouth, I'll shut up now."

And the bookstore owner said, "No, no, tell me more."

And so Nick told him more, and the bookstore owner admitted as he dropped Nick off, "I thought it was you yourself that you were describing."

Nick was astonished. And also taken aback. He hurried to assure the bookstore owner that he was no dancer. He was a stone builder, a builder of walls. He wished he could bring the store owner to one, to let him kick it and see it was real.

Skepticism played in the bookstore owner's face, as he thanked Nick for his companionship. He wished Nick well, and hoped that someday he might again see his dancer.

"And," he added, as Nick shut the door, "if you are ever in Kittery, please stop by my shop."

He drove off, and Nick laughed aloud. The serenity and certainty returned to him. He walked with a jaunty step down the rutted dirt road toward the Lady Blanche house. Everything seemed familiar and reassuring. The whole world seemed in bloom.

Up the driveway stood his pickup, solid and loaded with bits and flecks of stone.

The bookstore owner had not understood me, Nick thought. He had not believed a word. But this was fine. Nick had no interest in being understood widely, by everyone. For that kind of understanding, he couldn't give a damn.

What mattered were those few to whom he owed obligations. Including the obligation he owed to himself. And to Una.

It mattered deeply that she understand. As he knew she would.

Under that hard exterior was a woman with a firm sense of justice and an appreciation for truth and what mattered in life.

She was in the side room, which was nearly finished. Her laptop was set up on a card table and she sat before it, hammering away at the keys. She looked up as he entered. An instinctive smile crossed her face and then she looked away. She was resigned. Calm even.

"How did it go?"

He said nothing. Only took her hand as if she was a bride and he was going to slip a ring onto that finger. Together they stood and walked to the great glass walls of the library and looked out.

She allowed herself to be gathered in his arms. How small she was. Brent was no giant, but he was hard, hard like boys were supposed to be hard, and she was a delicate bird, light-boned, feathery.

He put his face in her hair.

"Do you have anything to tell me?" she asked.

Nick smiled in her face.

"I do, my dear. I really do."

CHAPTER 17

When Brent arrived home that morning, he refused to acknowledge Mrs. Sawyer's quizzical looks. He was dizzy with hunger, but he took only her coffee and retreated to the room where he had spent the whole summer.

He began to pack. It was a relief to be leaving. The last thing he needed was his mother to get all pitiful and sorry for him; that would make him break down and cry again. And he didn't need that.

After a suitable interval, she appeared in the doorway to his bedroom. Her saucer was flat in one hand, and she observed him over the brim of her teacup as she took a sip.

"Not like Nick to fail to show up, is it?" she said.

"I don't know," Brent said. Irritated. Solemn. "I don't know Nick at all."

"You seemed to know all about him yesterday. Can he have changed that much over night?"

Brent shrugged. "Things change. People change. Except me. I'm the only one who always seems to stay the same. Doing the same dumb things over and over." He looked up at his mother, who he knew would not be impressed by his pity-party. "I don't know, Ma. What difference does it make? A hundred years from now, it won't matter. Nothing's permanent."

"No," she agreed firmly. "Neither permanent, nor unending. Not even a stone wall. There's always a way around it. Or over it."

"Or through it," Brent added and hurled another pair of shorts into his bag. He would like to have bulldozed through Nick at that moment.

"Or through it. And just because it's built doesn't mean you cannot take it down."

"Fair enough, Mom. I get the picture. Enough with the parables, already, OK?"

"I'm not sure you do get the picture, Brent Sawyer." She let her words sink in and then asked in a different tone, "How long will you be gone?"

"Bobby said he'd be no more than a week. And I'll be right over by Sabbaday Lake if you need me. Just come on by."

"Are you sure that what you need is to be alone, Brent?"

"I'm not shutting myself away, Ma. Just house-sitting, doing Bobby a favor! I'd be doing this anyhow. It has nothing to do with Nick."

He knew this was not true. He *was* shutting himself away. To let the wound heal.

Mrs. Sawyer knew it, too. But she had been a mother long enough to know her son would resist being told the obvious truth and so she let him go.

Bobby's parents' house proved comforting in its familiarity. And it was blessedly quiet. Brent had to answer neither the phone nor the bell. His only obligation was simply to exist, to read, sip wine, and mull the future. The return to the city. The start of his new life.

Brent explored all the old places he and Bobby had hung out together when they were kids. He lingered in Bobby's room, where they had stolen their first sexual experience fifteen years before. Brent was not entirely unmoved. His heart was not made of stone. Never would be. However many times it was broken.

In the late afternoons and mornings, Brent sat on the back porch of Bobby's parents' house. From there, he could see directly across the lake to Mrs. Sawyer's camp, tucked away in the grove of pines.

It seemed strange to be looking at the world this way, as if he had stepped away from his own life and could now see it from a different perspective.

The neighbors were circumspect. Some nodded or waved from a distance. Brent wondered if they knew who he was, and whether they recognized him. Whether they minded his strutting around in his boxers. He wondered if they knew he was gay, if they knew he was a dancer. If they knew he had just got the crap fucked out of him by a man that was going to marry a woman and would never tell Brent that he loved him.

Probably not. Nobody ever knew what was going on beneath the surface. No one really wanted to know. This was what his sister Heidi had been trying to tell him. Don't waste your time trying to figure it out. Deal with what's on the surface.

On the third or fourth day—he had lost count—Brent dragged a canoe out from the garage and launched it out on to the lake at dawn. He had never been much of a boatsman—he had always preferred being *in* the water, trusting his own body to work out its rhythms against the water without the intercession of paddle and hull. But now it seemed right to try something different.

The water at dawn was dead calm. A fog was already thinning under the hot sun. At the high point of the stroke, the water dripped from his paddle like candle wax.

Brent set his paddle across his lap and the canoe continued forward on its own, unguided by anything but momentum. He leaned over the edge and peered down into the water. He imagined a different world, other people who had lived in this place before Brent. Long before Brent. It made him strangely resentful, as if their having been here first deprived him of a claim to discovery. A place that belonged to him alone.

Brent let one of his hands trail along the side of the canoe. He kept his eyes locked on a spot beneath the water, where he saw and lost silver shadows of swimming fish against the muck, like glimpses of true feelings.

The water was absolutely clear. Sabbaday Lake was famous for its clarity. Even a dog could see beneath, and he remembered their pet Labrador trotting back and forth on the dock tracing the progress of a school of smelts beneath the water before he finally jumped in and scattered them, snapping at the clear water.

Looking back on the past few weeks, Brent thought he could see with more clarity, too. He realized that he had hoped Nick would be so overpowered by their coupling that love would come pouring out of him, no matter how he tried to stop it. He had been so sure that Nick was capable of love, that he would be unable to stop it.

Brent looked again into the bottom of the lake. He fervently conjured another world among the tangled branches on the lake bottom, a world on the other side of the surface, looking back. It was a much different, fairy tale world, the world he had expected to unfold when he was a boy. The true love he had thought hopeless but had dreamed of endlessly.

He thought: *how did I end up here on the loveless side?*

It was a good hard row from one side of the lake to the other, but he made it in twenty-five minutes. He skirted his own shore, looking for any sign of life. The camp was quiet. So quiet he could hear the pitch putter from the trees to the pine bed. A loon called, close at hand.

It was good, he thought, to come back where he had started. To see how far he had come. It was a good foundation, he had. Strong family. On it, he wanted to build a house. A fortress made of Nick. In which he wanted to live, safely, with his knight.

The sadness he felt then was sweet, like the lake suffused with soft light after the sun had set. He set back again toward the opposite shore. His muscles felt capable and strong.

When Brent again beached the canoe in the sandy cove beneath Bobby's parents' house, he was startled by the sound of shouts and pounding.

What in God's name...?

He crept up the sand- and pine-scattered beach and traced the noise out to the front of the house. Cautiously, Brent peered around the corner through the branches of a lilac tree.

Nick was on the stoop. Every vein in his biceps stood out in stark relief.

Instinctively, Brent drew back around the corner of the house. His heart was pounding.

Then he thought: *what do I care if Nick sees me? Fuck 'im.*

Again, he peered around the corner. Again, Nick raised his fist and pounded on the front door as if he would break it down. He ceased pounding and stepped back, eyes scanning for movement at the windows.

"I know you're in there!" he shouted.

Brent stifled a laugh. *Well, so much for what you know, Nick. You don't know dick, my friend.*

For a moment, he debated confronting him, but then decided he did not need the grief.

Brent thought: *After a while, Nick will go away.*

He slipped in at the side door and began to make breakfast. He took his time. But Nick did not go away. He continued to shout, increasing in volume and persistence, and stalking around the house with the air of a hunted animal. After a while, it began to get on Brent's nerves, shredding the calm he had achieved that morning.

He marched to the front door and threw it open, startling Nick in mid-pound, so that he jumped back with fists raised, in a weird combination of aggression and flight.

"You're going to wake the neighbors," Brent said calmly. Firmly. The way you would reason with modern children.

"I need to talk to you."

"So…. talk. Who's stopping you?"

"Can I come in?"

Brent stepped aside. It was like opening the door to a hurricane. Nick stormed in, reached the far wall and stormed back to where Brent stood.

"You might want to calm down," Brent suggested mildly. "Have you considered Valium?"

Nick would not be calm. His voice was as loud as if he were drunk. It carried over the lake and echoed back to them after a while. It filled the room.

"Let's try using our indoor voices, shall we?" Brent suggested.

Nick was heedless. His eyes jumped from place to place, as if he expected the house to be exuding vermin from every crack and corner.

"I haven't slept in 72 hours," he said, speaking in a rush. "I went all the way down to your apartment in the city. Scared the hell out of someone there."

I bet you did, Brent thought ruefully. 195 rock-hard pounds of bellowing manhood—surprised he had not got arrested.

"I can't believe you left me behind. What was that all about? Was I not what you expected?"

"How'd you find me?" Brent interrupted. He was amazed at his ability to maintain his surface calm as his belly churned up like a Northeaster.

"Your mother told me what you were up to." The words were an accusation. Vindictive. Harsh.

"What I was up to? I wasn't aware I was up to anything at all."

"I can't understand how you could leave my bed for this...for this guy! It's..." Nick spluttered, unable to find the words for his outrage.

"What guy?"

"Don't play with me, Brent. You've done enough of that already."

"Playing with you?" he said. "Playing with *you?* That's a laugh. If there's anyone playing games here, it's..."

"I know whose house this is," Nick growled, cutting off Brent's retort. He seemed triumphant and pleased with himself, as if he had unraveled a great mystery despite all Brent's attempts to deceive him.

"I wasn't aware it was a secret, Nick. You checked the mailbox out front? How wonderful that you can read."

"Where is he?" Nick looked at Brent with utter loathing. Violent hatred. "Where is he?" Nick repeated.

Brent was not the slightest bit afraid of him.

"Are you smiling? Are you laughing at me?!" Nick demanded.

"No."

"Is this all some big joke to you? Here I thought you were beginning to grow up and that maybe, just maybe you were capable of some serious kind of...I must have been out of my mind."

He interrupted himself, pushing past Brent for the stairs, refusing to look Brent in the eyes. Refusing, Brent noticed, to touch him, to make any kind of physical contact.

He bounded up the stairs. At the landing, he actually opened the door of the linen closet at the top of the stairs as if to find someone hiding. Nick disappeared from view. Brent could hear him rummaging in the bedroom, muttering all manner of inaudible deprecations. Opening and closing drawers and closets.

Brent vaulted up the remaining steps to the second floor and chased Nick into the bathroom. Their voices echoed on the tiles.

"Nick, Nick, what...would you stand still for one minute!!" Brent shrieked.

Nick stood still, looking into the depths of the linen closet.

"What on earth are you doing?" Brent snapped. "What are you looking for?"

"Where's he hiding?"

"Who?"

"You know who!"

"Please tell me you're not talking about Bobby?"

"Why? or, why not? Is there more than one I have to worry about? Have you got boyfriends stashed all over?"

Brent stifled a laugh. "Nick..."

"If I know him, he'll be hiding under the bed, or under your skirts. God forbid he should stand up to anything or anybody."

A realization came across Brent as bright as the sun. Brent said, "You're crazy about me, aren't you, Nick?"

Nick froze.

Brent could not believe that he hadn't recognized it before. It was so obvious. So in-your-face. So sad.

He loves me too much, Brent thought.

"Instinct," Nick mumbled to himself, busy lecturing the

175

audience inside him. "Always go with the instinct. It's never wrong."

"It might be wrong..." Brent suggested.

Nick's red-rimmed eyes suddenly fixed on Brent's. He said, fiercely, "NEVER wrong." Nick threw up his hands. "I don't even know why I'm here," he said. "Why I care. If Bobby's what you want, then you deserve him. You want to be with a loser, that's your business."

The words stung. All the tenderness Brent's realization brought him went up like the flare of a match.

"Loser?! I knew it. I knew that's what you really think of me!"

"What do you mean?

"I know what you told Una—that I am a failed has been."

"Actually, I told her you had a lot of courage to walk away."

Bent opened his mouth to speak, but said nothing. He knew Nick was telling the truth.   Yet he could not shake the doubt: was he a loser like Una said?

Nick slammed the cellar door. He fumed, "I thought maybe it meant something to you to be together, but for you, Brent, it's just a fuck, right?"

"No, as a matter..."

"You're just like all the rest of them."

"I'm nothing like the rest of them!" Brent snapped. "My God, you're one to talk! You're fucking some woman, *marrying* some woman—" even in his fury Nick winced at the curses coming from Brent's mouth "—and you call me cheap? You're not just selling your sex, your selling your whole life. You think you've got it all under control, buddy...no. You're being controlled. That's right. Face it."

Nick knocked down a lamp that flashed blue. The blood left his face.

"As a matter of fact, I'm marrying no one," he said in a toneless, almost robotic voice. A deathly stillness fell over the room.

"I don't cheat," Nick said. "I told you that. I would never have slept with you if I were still engaged to Una."

"What are you talking about?"

"We had already broken it off. She was waiting for me to come home and tell her that you made me happy."

Brent was speechless.

"That's shocked you now, hasn't it? You didn't think you would ever meet an honest man?"

Brent floundered. His thoughts were racing like dogs around a track. He did not know what to think. He did not understand what he had heard. Hope and possibility and doom all fought for a place inside him.

"What would you know anyhow?" Nick said. "It probably doesn't mean anything to someone like you, anyhow. You'd drop your pants as soon as you'd take a breath. From one bed to another, and not a thought for the consequences."

Nick gestured at the house around them.

"As a matter of fact, Nicholas, I'm not shacking up with Bobby. Or anyone else. Bobby is in Burlington. He's trying to put his marriage back together, and God help her if the girl goes along with it. I'm just house-sitting."

It was Nick's turn to be speechless. The idea that Brent had other business in this house had never occurred to him. He opened his mouth to speak, but Brent held up a hand. A stop sign. His hand felt like it weighed a thousand pounds. It was time—beyond time—to put an end to all this surprise and counter-surprise. Brent could not live like this.

"You've been judging me and judging me and judging me since my sister got married. If you weren't so goddamn afraid, you might take a chance on believing something good about me instead of jumping to conclusions and immediately deciding I'm guilty of the worst sins you can think of. Well, maybe you don't know me, Nick. Maybe you can never know me. Because you're too damn afraid."

Brent was overwhelmed with a feeling of exhaustion. He added, "It's a shame, too, because I actually like you. And I may have been wrong about you and Una, but I still think I know you pretty well for such a short time. You, on the other hand, you're so goddamned anal, so stuck up on your high and mighty principles, and so determined to get up on your throne and judge us all, that you can't actually see anything around you.

"So you've been burned once, so what? Are the rest of us supposed to play cheer you up for the rest of your life? Fuck that, Mister Man.

"You know what, Nick? I'm not going to spend my life walking on eggshells because you're eyeing my every step looking for that moment I stumble. I don't need that. I don't deserve that. No one does. If I stumble, you should be there to catch me, not to gloat and blame and point out to everyone how right you were to suspect me from the get-go."

Brent felt as if he had more to say. Lifetimes more to say. But words failed him at this point.

"You should go now, before you do either of us any more pain. Build your stone walls. Hide in your castle. Go back to that woman, she would take you back, she doesn't care about anything but a green card, anyhow."

Even as he said these words, he knew they were not true. He was just saying them to make the inevitable break easier to take.

"I think it's lucky," Brent said quietly, "that we had this little blow up and learned what we think about each other. It'll save a lot of heartbreak down the road."

Brent looked Nick in the eye as he said this. And some small part of his heart hoped Nick would deny it. Would take him in his arms and refuse to take no for an answer. He wanted love to be stronger than petty feuds between proud men.

But Nick's pupils had narrowed. His eyes turned cold and hard as a pair of stones on the riverbed. Even if he had wanted to, Brent knew, Nick would never give in now, not in the heat of conflict. He had too much pride, and pride in his case won over love every time.

Brent took in the details of his face, the open collar, the heat that seemed to come out of his chest like a steam engine. Drank in the details because he never expected to see them again. They were just fodder for the scrapbook. Sepia tinted photographs of another time.

This is for the better, Brent told himself. *We would never be happy with one another.*

Brent tried to believe it. Tried to force himself to believe it. But already the regret hung on him like a suit of lead.

CHAPTER 18

It was three long days before Bobby returned from his mission to save his marriage. The longest days in the history of the world. Brent's watch seemed to have come to a complete stop. He would finish his coffee and think it was noontime, only to find that it was hardly a minute after seven a.m.

A New England cold front set in and chased away the August heat. Brent's very chilly and desolate, as if he was living in the northern tundra on a supply of rapidly diminishing food. He did not eat or care to eat. He took books from the shelves and they were mere props. Not one word on the page made any sense to him. Nothing made sense to him.

What a great mystery Nick was. No one in his life had so intrigued Brent and so infuriated him. So infatuated him. Giving his body to Nick felt like he had placed himself in the hands of his destined caretaker, the person appointed to play that role.

And, similarly, he had felt that Nick had come home when he came into Brent's presence. He had felt these things, he was sure. It was undeniable. It was the only thing that made sense in Brent's heart of hearts, where true understanding is, not clouded by the thoughts that plague men's minds.

Cold fog socked in the cabin half the morning. The lake's banks disappeared. He could see only a patch of still water stretching at best ten feet from his own shore. And then nothing.

Brent grew furious with Nick. Why could he not see just how good it could have been between them? If only Nick had relinquished that ferocious pride. If only he had seen that there were obligations higher than his promises and plans. Obligations to himself. To Brent. To something greater than both of them.

And then his fury would turn on himself. He ransacked the events of the last few days as if they were a closet jammed full of stashed gold. Where had he gone wrong? How could he have been nicer? Sweeter? More irresistible?

At the loneliest times, Brent lay out on the rocks by the beach and stared up into the passing clouds. The stones bit into his back and bones. They were cold and damp.

But Brent imagined that this was what it must feel like to be loved on one of stone's walls. Sex on the rocks, he thought. With stones pressing into his kidneys, abrading his flesh, the whole weight of stone on top of him.

He imagined Nick forcing back his head for a kiss, a finger beneath Brent's chin, and just before their lips touched the soft crack of Brent's skull on stone, not painful, just dull, and then tongue in his mouth obliterating any pain or thought whatever. He would be pummeled. Pumiced. He would have bruises all over and he would know he was alive.

He masturbated there in the great outdoors and the jizz spilled over his belly and seemed to go instantly cold.

Where was Bobby? Brent wondered. Why had he not called? When would he come back?

Brent returned to the bedroom mirror again and again and inspected himself mercilessly at close range. He thought he detected signs of age. The first glimpse of crow's feet. The first gray hairs. Flab. Wrinkles. Sagging. Soon they would have him in a wheel chair and he would be lecturing anybody who would listen that he used to be pretty once.

When feeling sorry for himself itself got old and tired, Brent looked in the mirror again and assured his reflection there would be plenty of other men in his life besides Nick. Life was long. He knew he could drive to New York this very instant and find himself a hundred-thousand eligible gay men.

But a hundred-thousand did not seem enough. Indeed, the city seemed empty, more sparsely populated than Holmstead County itself.

Life was long, Brent thought ruefully. Too long.

Where was the evidence that there were all these wonderful men out there? Brent could only base it on his own experience. The law of numbers did not seem to hold true.

In all Brent's life, he had experienced a spark this powerful with just one person—Nick. It seemed impossible to have to wait and hope for lightning to strike twice.

Bobby's return was triumphant and sudden. He bounded through the door with a shit-eating grin, and beelined for the fridge for a can of beer.

"Hey-hey," he called out, positively buoyant. He immediately began relating the success of his efforts to patch up his marriage. His wife still loved him, and all was right in the world.

Brent stared at Bobby with amazement. He was a creature from another planet. An alien. Bobby seemed to be tone deaf, unable to feel, hear, sense the desolation in this cabin that Brent had been inhabiting for the last thousand days. Or so.

Alone with the desolation. Dancing with it.

It was so patently unfair. Salt in Brent's wounds. That this bumbling straight idiot Brent had once loved could contrive to somehow keep his love intact! Without any particular talent. Or strength of character. And only the smallest modicum of half-hearted, dimestore effort that would peter out in a month's time.

Bobby hadn't a grain of higher feeling. No sense of obligation. None of Nick's nobility.

He had acted, Brent thought, purely out of desperation. Desperate that he would not be like me. Not gay. Not lonely.

Bobby rattled on and Brent stopped listening. He watched Bobby speak, watched his mouth move, heard a noise from it. But he made no attempt to parse or understand the words. He was alienated entirely from Bobby. They lived in two different worlds.

Only Nick himself might understand what Brent was feeling. Only Nick himself. And Nick, Brent thought, would not be so ungenerous.

Brent caught himself looking at Bobby with the kind of distaste with which he would regard something caught on his shoe.

Relax, he told himself. *Lord knows, it's not Bobby's fault.*

Brent was just using Bobby's happiness to accentuate his own misery. Bobby was not to blame. Nick was not to blame. There may be, Brent thought, no blame to be had. Which was more than a bitchy gay man could abide. He *needed* someone or something to blame. What fun was it if there was no one on whom to take out his ire and use as a scratching post?

At the first sign of a break in Bobby's monologue, Brent fled. He stopped first at Heidi's house.

"I can see you haven't eaten in days," she said with thorough disapproval.

"You know us anorexic gay men," Brent said. He tried to put cheer into the quip, but could not.

He kept forcing himself to try to accept the conclusion: his husband was someone else. Not Nick. He had to accept this fact. Repeat it to himself ten times in the morning and ten times at night. Write it on the blackboard after school.

As close as it had seemed, Nick was not the man.

And had it even been close? Had he been fooling himself in the weakness of his career change and the marriage of his favorite sister and a dose of overactive hormones?

Pick up the pieces, he told himself. There was a time for everything, including desolation.

But there is also a time to move on.

To Heidi, Brent confessed, "You were right, I ruined it."

"Una is going to get her green card anyway. It seems there's an amnesty program they looked into. She and I just went down to the federal immigration office. It covers her, and her kids. And best of all, it means she's going to be able to get a job...."

"Hmm. Well, I guess that's good. Not everyone has to suffer."

"You do." Heidi smiled. "Sometimes I think you like to suffer a little bit. Like it's not worth it unless you do. Isn't that what you used to say about dancing when you came home with those messed up feet, bruised and calloused?"

Brent sniffed. His own stoicism wasn't worth much to him now and did not impress him. But he dared to ask the question that had been plaguing him.

"Do you think it was courageous of me to walk away from dancing?"

She did not hesitate in her reply. "It's just what I would expect of you. You're not going to be satisfied with doing it halfway or half as well."

Brent nodded, in quiet satisfaction at this answer.

"But I'm glad you didn't stop dancing altogether," she added. "It would have been a shame to have missed you doing that at my wedding."

It was near the end of summer now. The days were golden and warm, but shorter now. The season had started a long glide toward winter, and Brent was soon to be returning to the city. He packed away his summer clothes.

The night before his departure, Mrs. Sawyer summoned all Brent's sisters and their children for a last family get-together. Mrs. Sawyer fired up the grill and seared a mountain of fresh vegetables and beef. There was cake and ice cream, and a dozen rambunctious kids.

Heidi plopped down next to Brent in one of the wicker chairs on the porch. "You aren't going to leave here without seeing Nick, are you?"

Brent did not look at her. "Who's Nick?"

"Come on, Brent..."

"Of course I'm not going to see Nick. Are you kidding?"

"You guys are made for each other."

"Made to kill each other. Let him come to me if he wants to say good bye."

"Would you be nice to him if he did?"

"No."

Heidi threw her hands up in disgust. "You two are impossible!

185

Goddamn egos. I can't for the life of me figure out why I like men at all."

"Maybe you've just got a thing for dick," Brent suggested mildly.

"Maybe you'd like to shut your mouth around the kids if you'd like to keep yours," Heidi shot back.

Brent laughed. "OK. We're even."

"Oh no we're not, Brent Sawyer, I am not done with you yet." Heidi gave him a long meaningful look.

Brent's sister Martha barged into the kitchen. She begged Brent to wear his clock-face costume one more time. "The kids have been pestering me," she explained. "You've got to do me this favor. This is how they're going to remember this summer, I promise."

"The clock costume? Again?"

"It's about time you did," she said. Her face brightened like a sun. "Get it? About 'time' you did? 'time'—get it? Clocks?"

Brent groaned. "I got it."

"Come on! Are you going to disappoint the kids?"

"Hey, am I the one who's breeding? Am I responsible for your kids?"

"Absolutely," Heidi chimed in. "You're the gay uncle. Every kid needs one."

"And I think," Martha added, "you'd start breeding, if you had the right man."

She and Heidi shared a conspiratorial look that Brent did not understand.

"Don't count on it, sister," Brent warned with his usual confident bravura, "it's hard to get a sitter when you're at the dance club until four a.m."

"You talk a tough game, Brent, but we know you, remember? We're your sisters."

Heidi added, "You'll get bored of that life sooner or later."

Brent growled dismissively at the tag-team approach. Reluctantly, he allowed his sisters to persuade him into his giant clock face, which he had put away in the back of his closet reluctant to throw it away.

"OK, OK," he grumbled, "I'll get into the costume, you witches. You don't have to threaten me with turning straight. Or worse yet, old."

While his sisters and mother sat on the porch, Brent raced around the backyard with the kids, his clock face slapping in the breeze, impossible to read the time. He led them on a jaunt through the woods and along the stone wall Nick had completed, working fourteen hours a day when Brent was at Bobby's.

They took turns chasing each other here and there. One moment Brent was the bad guy, the next it was the mob of kids. Along riverbanks and woods and on logs over streams and through the long uncut grass of the meadows. An ever-changing scene.

When the children began to tire, Brent turned back toward the house. Summoning a last bit of energy from his worn out legs, he sprinted the last hundred yards. He came sailing breathlessly around the corner of the house, pursued by a mob of screaming kids—and stopped in his tracks.

There was a costumed figure in the front yard bearing down on him, dressed from head to foot in a gorilla suit, which must have been roasting hot in the late August heat.

It was impossible to doubt who was inside. His size alone gave him away. That and the three clean Irish faces that were gathered around his legs—Una's three children.

Before Brent's mind had even made the connection, his heart had started pounding in immediate bodily recognition.

You are what you are, Brent thought. *You can't hide your essential being.*

Before they could speak to one another, Brent was overtaken by a wave of screaming children—some from behind him, the rest Una's little sprites. They brought Brent down in the grass, tickling and screaming. For a moment, Nick watched and then surrendered his dignity.

He leapt into the fray. Both sets of children were delighted to have a fresh victim, and they leaped on him gladly. When wrestling proved boring and the kids were tired of chasing and wanted to be chased, Nick obliged them, running around the backyard and tripping all over himself because the eye holes did not quite fit his head.

Brent sat cross-legged on the grass. He was trying to rehabilitate what was left of the clock costume. The hands were broken off and the clock face was creased and bent. He felt compelled to fix them and put it all to right.

Brent's sisters and mother had disappeared from the porch. He could see them holed up at the kitchen window, craning necks and trying to see the spectacle outside.

He glanced over at Nick, who was still busy chasing children, then roused himself and pursued the ladies inside.

"Sorry to spoil your fun," Brent said. "I'm not doing this."

They all jumped. They had not expected him to come inside.

"What are you doing in here?" Heidi asked.

"Get him out of here," Brent says to his sister. "I don't want to talk with him."

Brent meant it. He swore he did. He would not be charmed by these games with the kids. Or by his sisters' shenanigans. It was over between him and Nick.

But the anger he had expected and even hoped to feel did not seize him. Instead, he found the wrong kinds of feelings welling up—hope and desire and sadness. And forgiveness.

Brent was embarrassed at himself for giving these feelings reign. For even feeling them at all. He should hate Nick. He should be tired of all this. The time had passed for them. Their moment—if any—was in the past.

Brent threw an accusing look at his sisters. Three of them looked away, faces filled with...what? Did he detect shame? Compassion?

Not at all. It was delighted guilt that lit up their faces. The laughter they had tried to contain spilled through the hands with which they tried to stifle it.

When they could bear it no more, they fell against one another laughing.

Adam appeared from the next room with his own big grin. It seemed that even he was in on the joke.

"Let's go outside, dude. With a quickness. I'll get the kids. You get the man. Deal?"

When Brent hesitated, Heidi said, "Well, you didn't think he was actually going to give up on you that easily, did you?"

Adam dragged Brent through the door.

Outside, Nick had removed his mask and the top half of his gorilla suit and was waiting for him in a wife-beater. His biceps and shoulders bulged and his lats were like wings.

Adam propelled Brent into confrontation with him and then, as promised, took his turn diving among up the gaping children.

"What's up with the gorilla suit?" Brent said for lack of anything better to say.

Nick blushed. "It was the only thing they had my size."

He smiled grimly.

Both of them were itching suddenly to be rid of this audience of siblings and parents and little kids. To be quietly away.

What they would do there—away—Brent hadn't a clue.

Too much had been said between them already. And yet not enough. Silence was a good compromise. It seemed to fill and nourish Brent's heart.

Sensing the awkwardness, Adam rounded up the children and led them away.

"What a good kid he is!" Brent said, looking after him. "So sensitive. You'd almost think he was gay." Brent smiled at Nick. "I brought that kid up right."

"You've got a good family."

"Great family."

"Tough family. They've been on my ass for the past two weeks."

"Finally made you give in?"

"Finally gave me the courage."

Brent doubted that Nick had ever in his life been held back by lack of courage. In fact, it would have been better if Nick was not quite so damn sure of himself as he stood there. He showed no doubts that he could have Brent now. Would have Brent. That showing up was enough.

This made Brent want to scream and rebel just to prove that he was not so easily taken. He began to rear back his shoulders when he heard from the window above Heidi's scolding voice: "Don't you even begin to think of getting all high and mighty and unavailable, little brother. I'll take you into the back room and spank you."

Nick raised his hand. "May I do the honors?"

They all laughed, except Brent. Who, uncharacteristically, blushed.

He turned to his audience in the windows.

"All right, witches, don't you think you've done enough damage already. Put away your catnip and eye of newt and go back to breeding, or something, wouldja?"

Brent reached for Nick's hand. He felt a tremor run through it at his touch. And he wondered whether Nick was indeed as sure of himself as he seemed.

"Una let you take care of the children?"

"Of course," Nick said. "It's only her I'm not marrying. Nothing to stop me from being a friend to the little ones, is there?"

"N-no."

"Once I love someone, I don't let them go that easily. They'll always be a part of my life."

Nick gave Brent a look that went through him like a sheet of flame.

Brent led him to the stone wall Nick had built. He glanced back toward the house, where the window was crowded with familiar, disobedient faces.

Brent released Nick's hand, hopped the wall, and crouched in the little depression on the far side where they could not be seen.

Nick followed obligingly.

The first thing he said was, "Marrying someone you don't love is a terrible thing. Not when there's someone else you're supposed to be spending your life with."

His eyes did not leave Brent's face. They were shining, hungry, yearning. And expectant.

To be the object of such an appetite—wasn't that all Brent had ever wanted? And yet it was scary to confront, to see it here in a face inches from his own. A magnificent handsome face. A man in love with him.

"Una and I have a very special relationship. She is a wonderful mother. She cares for me deeply. That's why she tried so hard to scare you off. In part because she wanted to scare you off, to protect her and the children. In part, to protect me. To make sure you were worthy of me, in her eyes. Do you understand?"

Brent nodded. "I heard she might get a job, too."

"Remember that client I introduced you to? Now that Una's going to have a green card, he's going to be able to find a position for her in one of his companies."

"Good work sometimes pays off in unexpected ways."

Nick squeezed Brent's hand. "Amen," he whispered.

Brent felt suddenly shy and panicky. His eyes were like squirrels, zippering back and forth, meeting Nick's eyes, then looking away, then back again.

"I love you," Nick said. He kissed Brent, not on the lips, but on the forehead. And it seemed the prelude to a thousand million kisses, the teasing sign of what was to come.

There was an immediate surge in Brent's belly. The lick of Nick's lips quickened Brent's loins.

"I promised your sisters I would not let any more nonsense come between us," Nick said. "You know I can keep a promise."

Brent stared at him. He was perplexed by all the questions that ran through his head, and the audience behind the curtain of stone, the chorus of sisters, clustered one on top of the other in the window. Brent knew they would be smiling, congratulating themselves, pleased at what they had wrought and would no doubt forever take credit for.

They had it easy, Brent thought. They do not have to figure out how to make it work for years and years and years with this infuriating beautiful passionate man.

Brent looked back in Nick's face. The broad honest forehead. The wise beguiling eyes that rarely gave up their secrets. The full lips, still shining from a touch of his tongue. The firm jaw line, which seemed to define all the strength in the man's body.

Nick squeezed Brent's hand. He was as excited as a child.

Brent suddenly thought he knew nothing about this man. Next to nothing. But he was insatiably curious to find out. Insatiably curious to find out.

Because he knew the things that mattered—the fineness of his character, his courage, and his honor. He had, he thought, always known these things about Nick, from before he even met them. They were the stuff of Brent's dreams.

And Brent knew the rest of his life would be learning what else made up Nick. Where he came from and what he had done and where he was going.

There was so much to do together. So much to create. A castle to build.

What would it mean? Where would they live? There were not a lot of stone walls to build in the city. There weren't many dance venues in Holmstead County that needed an old has-been as a director.

Too many questions rushed through Brent's head. But they were followed by a closing certainty, certain as stone, that he and Nick would work all these details out. Which were unimportant. The vows he had made never to move home were nothing next to the vows he would make with Nick, and Nick had the same feeling.

Brent leaned back against the wall Nick had built. A firm foundation that would last for a hundred years.

Imagine how bored I would have been with a man like Bobby, Brent thought, as Nick's arms closed about him, a perfect fit under August sun. The scruff of his chin, the sweat of his chest, the swell of his muscles—he had obviously been working before he came to the party, and Brent was pleased at his sense of duty. And the greater courage it took to forgo pride for love. He loved him for his coming here when Brent had convinced himself—almost—to give up.

If there was anything to love most in a man, it was this kind of courage. That would not diminish and would never turn away, and centuries from then people would look back with awe at what they had built.